# PERFECT___ _____

## Perfectly Series Book 3

## LINDA O'CONNOR

Keep lovin'!
Keep laughin'!
Linda

inter**Lock**
**PUBLISHING**

PERFECTLY PLANNED

Copyright©2015

LINDA O'CONNOR

Cover Design by Rae Monet, Inc.
Published in Canada by Interlock Publishing
InterlockPublish@gmail.com

Library and Archives Canada Cataloguing in Publication

O'Connor, Linda A., author
         Perfectly planned / Linda O'Connor.

(Perfectly series ; book 3)
Issued in print and electronic formats.
ISBN 978-0-9949173-1-7 (paperback).--ISBN 978-0-9949173-0-0 (pdf)

         I. Title.

PS8629.C652P47 2015          C813'.6          C2015-906955-6
                                               C2015-906956-4

*To Brian Cross and the members of the OPP TRU team ~ who risk their lives to keep us safe.*

Other Books in the Perfectly Series:

Perfectly Honest
Perfectly Reasonable

# Acknowledgements

Wow – book 3! This has been a thrilling journey, and I couldn't have done it without the support of my family and friends. I would like to thank Brian Cross for his patience in answering all of my questions – I think I owe you another dinner!

Special thanks to Ellie Barton, Shirley Baird, Linda Delve, Liesa Cross, Jeff Nelson, and George Eastwood – for their eagle eyes and thoughtful feedback!

Huge thanks to Rae Monet for the beautiful cover design.

Thank you from my heart to:
Brad, Tom, and Mark, who answer all my research questions and quietly promote my books;

my Mom, for all of her wonderful advice;

Karen Marcotte, artist of beautiful cards and my most avid supporter;

Lesley Rooke, for her positive voice and unwavering support;

and to everyone who read Perfectly Honest and Perfectly Reasonable and encouraged me along the way.

Here you have it – Perfectly Planned – another dream come true!

# **Chapter 1**

That was easy. Chloe Keay spun around in the office chair and smiled. Thank you, social media. Two new friends and plans for Friday night. How productive.

Her mouse hovered over her profile picture. She probably should update it. A year ago her hair had been flaming red. Gave her a homey Anne-of-Green-Gables look. Without the freckles. Or the pigtails. Or the round face and green eyes. She laughed. Yeah, she was nothing like Anne of Green Gables, but she had thought it suited Roger. She had been going for a wholesome 'let's start a family and settle by the water' kind of look. Turns out Roger was more of a 'live in a condo, travel, never have kids' kind of guy.

So.

Good-bye, Roger.

Hello, bleach blond hair. She glanced at her reflection on the computer screen. It kinda said come have my babies. Her gaze dropped lower to her chest. She smiled wryly. That definitely said come have my babies. How come that hadn't worked?

She shrugged. Didn't matter. She didn't need to impress anyone or send out a mating signal. She was done with all that.

Her thirtieth birthday was on the horizon, and the future was making history.

She had listened to the financial news every morning with Roger. (The relationship wasn't all a waste.) Not that she really cared about Dowel Jones, whoever he was, or the Toronto sock exchange (Really? Socks cost two dollars, buy new ones), but there was only so much chatter about painting you could do. Said Roger. She could chatter about painting all day. That's pretty much what she did. And now that her boss, Margo MacMillan, a.k.a. Sweetheart Smarty-pants, was back with a stethoscope around her neck after a year of painting full-time, Chloe talked about it even more. Homes, hotels, warehouses, any wall, any color, it all worked for her.

But with all the financial advice she was catching up on, she did notice one thing. The population was aging (Someone's just figuring that out?) and there wasn't going to be enough money in the pension plan. Hmmm. Apparently that was a problem. And not that she liked to think too far into the future, but it seemed you needed a retirement plan.

Not only was it 'highly recommended,' but, they stressed several days in a row, it had to be started by age thirty. Hmmm. Retirement plan at age thirty, who'd have thought?

Well, if that's what kept the big bean counters from *Money Market News* up at night, she'd better sit up and listen.

She never had to worry about what to do with her 'disposable income.' Sheez. She disposed of it. It wasn't that hard. (She should do a podcast or two for them.) "Don't spend what you don't have," her mom always said. "Debt isn't your friend," her dad would chip in.

Her parents, sixty-nine, turning seventy in a week, shared the same birthday and the same financial vision. They were thrifty, but knew they needed more. Their retirement plan was simple—have six children. There was bound to be a high achiever among them.

They were right. Dale, the eldest, was a lawyer. Pamela, number two, a nurse. Devon, number three, a dentist. April was an electrical engineer. She painted houses and Cory, her twin, was a plumber.

For pretty much everything her parents needed, from house repairs to health questions, they had a child on speed-dial. And bonus, funds flowed freely to pay for their place in a retirement home.

Perfectly planned.

That's the kind of retirement plan she was after. Maybe not six kids. Six was a bit of a handful, especially flying solo. But she could handle one, at least to begin with.

It would've been easier with Roger, but oh well, on to Plan B.

Sperm bank.

She had been poked and prodded and deemed a healthy receptacle.

But, oh how to choose which little swimmers to let loose? She needed smart (had to earn the big bucks), features similar to hers (hair color notwithstanding), family oriented (obviously had to love their momma), and not too nasally a voice (very annoying). They needed to be screened for reverse traits—ones that would make her wish she could reverse the whole process.

She needed more than the measly amount of info available online.

No problem. She had applied for a job as a weekend receptionist at the sperm bank, interviewed quite successfully (naturally), and waited patiently while they narrowed down their selection.

She had started three weeks ago.

The job was straightforward, certainly not as creative as painting. In fact, it was kinda slow. She liked the music in the waiting room, though, especially with her mouse clicking. She could get quite a beat going. Left click. Right click. Left-right-right click. She could see it catching on. In fact, it should be posted on YouTube because it'd give her something to watch at work, too.

She hadn't lost sight of her plan, but it wasn't obvious where all the data was stored. She had opened several files, but it wasn't until she rocked and clicked to The Jaded Gentlemen, that lo and behold, the folder popped up.

Now, she wasn't a computer genius or anything, but who uses 1234 as their password? You'd think all that confidential information about sperm donors would be behind a bigger firewall. Nope.

So, her two top matches now had names.

4652. Ripley Logan

2485. Jared Clayton

A few social media clicks later, and voilà, she set up friend requests with both.

Even better, it looked like Ripley's baseball team had a rain-date game on Friday, seven o'clock, right here in Rivermede at Fairfield Park.

He was sporty. She clicked a happy beat.

She could go to the game and check him out. Try to learn more about him, but keep it quiet, fly under the radar.

She spun around in her chair and smiled. Perfect.

Looking back at the screen, she hovered the cursor over her profile picture. Redhead or blond?

What did that financial guru say? Plan carefully, go slowly, get the core established before exploring any specific tactical shifts.

Hmmm. Sounded like the redheaded photo should stay a little longer.

# Chapter 2

Chloe pulled into the parking lot at Fairfield Park at seven thirty on Friday evening and had her pick of parking spots. Surprisingly, since the park was actually quite busy. The baseball game was underway on the diamond in front of the parking lot. The stands on the right, along the third baseline, were almost full. Across the field, in a playground beyond home plate, adults watched the game as they pushed little ones on swings. More children (yes, all adequately supervised) made use of a giant play structure complete with climbing rungs and a slide.

A lot of people out enjoying the balmy August weather. They'd had an unusually rainy July, which had been good for turning the brown grass of summer a lush green. But now, in the third week of August, they'd had nothing but sunny days and warmer-than-average evenings.

Chloe grabbed a baseball cap and light jacket from the passenger seat of her car. She tugged on the hat and pulled her ponytail through the back. She adjusted her sunglasses, loving the extra daylight that made them necessary. After locking the car, she wandered over to the stands.

"Strike three. You're out." The umpire signaled the call as Chloe sat down. Fans clapped and the team in the outfield jogged toward the dugout. Players from the opposite dugout slipped on baseball caps as they ran out onto the field.

Chloe squinted and tried to read the third baseman's jersey. Poppa Pete's Knuckleballs. Ripley Logan's team must be at bat because his posted pictures were all about the Tried and TRU. She wrinkled her nose. Hopefully, that wasn't a sexual reference.

The first batter up had very good form. Well-toned arms, nice butt. Got a two base hit. She wondered if he donated sperm.

The second batter struck out. He had very skinny legs. Pass.

The third batter sauntered out like he owned the field. All the outfielders backed up.

"Bring me home, Rip," shouted the player at second base, clapping his hands.

"Let'er rip," added a voice from the dugout.

"Get'em on the board," a silver-haired gentleman sitting beside Chloe called out. A few fans joined the clapping.

Rip. Ripley Logan. Sounds like my man, Chloe thought and sat a little straighter. He was very attractive. A solid twelve out of ten. The navy T-shirt stretched across his broad chest and flat abdomen. Shorts showed off his muscular legs, and when he stuck out his butt to swing, Chloe raised her eyebrows. She could live with that.

He swung the bat on the first pitch and connected with the ball. It cracked off the bat and sailed into left field. Ripley dropped the bat and sprinted.

Heaven. A little taste of heaven on earth.

He was so pretty. Fluid, graceful, lightning fast. The player on second made it home, and Ripley made it to third. A silly man standing near the third base stopped him. Really, it was poetry in motion. Why would you stop that? Chloe shook her head.

It took two more batters to bring Ripley home. The inning ended and the Tried and TRU were up two runs.

She followed Ripley as the inning changed and watched him walk over to cover first base. He played it well. Very good hand-eye coordination. Nice long reach. Quick reflexes. Reasonable shoe size. Beautiful smile. Looked like he had straight teeth, but she'd really have to get closer to assess. All in all, she was pretty pleased. He hadn't said enough to check for the nasally voice, but it was looking positive.

She loved the atmosphere at the game. Fans clapped and stood with each exciting play. Between innings, music blared over the loud speakers. She really got into rooting for the Tried and TRU, and when the music played she sang along.

"Carrots and biscuits. Every day." She loved that song. It was so healthy. She joined in at the top of her lungs, but stopped when the gentleman beside her gave her an odd look.

"What?" she asked.

"Isn't that supposed to be 'Takin' Care of Business'?" he said, shaking his head.

'Taking Care of Business?' What kind of health food message was that? She frowned at her neighbor, who had shifted his attention back to the game.

After seven innings, Chloe went in search of popcorn. Actually, she had a craving for peanuts and Cracker Jack, but the canteen was limited to plain or buttered popcorn. No peanuts, the woman said with a horrified expression, mumbling something about risk and high taxes.

Whatever. Chloe took the bag of popcorn and found a seat in the stands closer to the Tried and TRU dugout. And the waves of radiating testosterone.

Really, with the exception of Skinny Legs, there was a stellar choice of sperm in that dugout. She munched the popcorn. Her talents were wasted as a receptionist at the sperm bank. They should hire her to recruit donors. She'd found a gold mine.

At the top of the ninth, Ripley came up to bat again.

Chloe smiled and set the popcorn bag down, ready to clap.

The pitcher wound up, and Ripley connected with the sweet spot. The ball soared in the air. The infield and outfield watched as the ball arced over them toward the parking lot.

Chloe sat straighter as the ball, almost in slow motion, fell dead center into the windshield of the only car parked in the north lot. The sound of glass shattering broke the silence.

"Who the hell parked there?"

Chloe looked over at Rip, a hand on his hip, a scowl on his face. A nasally voice wasn't going to be an issue.

# Chapter 3

"Congratulations on your win," Chloe said to Ripley. He's a tall one. She had to look up to catch his eye. Did she want her child towering over her? Hopefully height came from the mother.

He raised his eyebrows. "Thanks," he said dryly, glancing at her car. A web of cracked glass radiated from the hole in the center of the windshield.

Yes, straight teeth. He needed to smile more, though.

"Sorry about your windshield. You didn't see the sign?" He pointed to a small sign off to the right.

Brown eyes. That would be a dominant trait. Actually, they were more of a brown gray, quite mesmerizing really.

He gestured impatiently. Chloe glanced at the sign.

*Use south lot during games. Not responsible for property damage.*

"I did see that. That's why I parked here," she said.

"This is the north lot. The south lot is further . . . south."

"And I'm supposed to know that because . . ."

"Because most people know north from south."

"I am not most people," she said.

He glanced at her windshield and snorted. "Yeah, and now you have a uniquely smashed windshield. You have insurance to cover that?"

"No," she said, lifting her chin. "You're going to pay for it."

"No." He shook his head. "That's what 'not responsible for property damage' means."

"I don't think so. He who hits the ball is responsible for where the ball goes. It's section 7.2 of the Canadian Criminal Code," she said, crossing her fingers behind her back.

"Really? Section 7.2 of the Criminal Code. This is a criminal matter?"

"Yes," she said, with a confident nod. Her insurance rates were outrageously high. It was criminal. And she wasn't about to submit another claim and risk them going higher.

"Section 7.2. Committing an offense on an aircraft? That section 7.2?"

Uh-oh. He actually knew Section 7.2? "No. It's the part about willfully destroying property."

"Ohhhh," he said. "That 7.2. You mean Section 430 of the Criminal Code."

"Right." She cleared her throat. "I must have gotten them mixed up. Section 430. Of course."

"I didn't willfully destroy your property. It was an accident."

She gave him a pointed look. "Did you or did you not hit the ball as hard as you could in this direction to get a home run?"

He gave a short laugh and shook his head. "I don't think—"

"Just answer the question." Judge Judy used that line a lot.

He shrugged. "Yes. Yes I did," he said with a smile.

She nodded. "I rest my case. Willful destruction. How much time do you get if you don't pay up?"

"It's indictable to life imprisonment."

"Wow. Severe. You don't want that, do you?"

"No," he said with a laugh.

"I didn't think so. So, how do we go about this? You'll write me a blank check?" Actually, that wasn't a bad idea. She could get his handwriting analyzed. She knew someone who could do that.

"No."

She glanced at him. He smiled slightly (and boy with that five o'clock shadow, very sexy, high testosterone level—all good). But that was a pretty emphatic no. "What do you suggest?"

Rip looked down at the blue eyes set in a heart-shaped face and the blond ponytail poking out of the baseball cap. Her skin looked smooth and soft, and he almost reached out to touch it. Who was she? Why did she look familiar?

He mentally flipped through the wanted-person file in his head. No, it wasn't work related. But he'd seen that face recently.

His gaze dropped lower, and his body stirred. Curves in all the right places. More soft and smooth.

"Hey, buddy," she said, snapping her fingers. "Focus."

Rip jerked and felt his cheeks flush. "Sorry," he said stiffly. He cleared his throat. "Look, I can get this taken care of," he said, pointing to the windshield, "but it might have to wait until Monday."

She made a face. "What do I do in the meantime?"

"We can get it towed to the shop, and I can give you a lift home. Can you make do without a car for the weekend?"

She bit her lip. "Probably. You don't think I could drive it home? And bring it to the shop on Monday?"

He glanced over at the windshield. "Not unless you want a ticket for operating an unsafe vehicle."

"No, I don't." She sighed. "I suppose I could call a cab. I don't want to be a bother."

Rip laughed. Nailing him for the windshield repair wasn't a bother? He shrugged. "Let me get the tow truck organized and then you can decide. Driving you home isn't a problem."

He pulled out his cell phone and made a couple of phone calls. The first was for a tow truck. The second was to his friend who owned the garage. "Hey Smitty, it's Rip."

Smitty started laughing.

"You could at least wait until I tell you what it's for," Rip said.

"I can guess. You had a game tonight, right? I hope you won."

"Of course. Although it would've been cheaper to lose."

"Dent repair and windshield?"

"Just the windshield."

"Your aim is improving. What kind of car is it?"

"Looks like an older model Chevy. Let me ask." He held his phone away from his ear and turned to Chloe. "What type of car is it?"

"Seventy-four Camaro."

Rip nodded and spoke into the phone. "Yep. Seventies Camaro."

"Ouch. I'm not sure about the stock for that one. Those old vintage ones are harder to find. I could check into it first thing Monday, but that's the best I can do."

"Fair enough. I thought you were going away this weekend."

"Heading out the door now."

"I'll get it towed over—" Rip began.

Smitty's burst of laughter cut him off. "Must've been a good hit."

"Call me Monday," Rip said, ignoring him.

"Cheers."

The tow truck arrived as he finished the call.

"Hey, Sarge. How ya doin'? Are the vandals back?" the driver asked.

Rip shook his head. "Not this time. This was the price of a home run."

The driver grinned. "Did you win?"

"Damn right."

"All that matters." He worked quickly and had the car jacked up and ready to go. "Over to Smitty's?"

"Yes, sir. Thanks very much."

"Any time, Sarge. Any time." With a salute, the driver climbed in his truck and pulled away.

Chloe stood off to the side and eyed him as the tow truck pulled out. "Is your name Sarge?"

Rip laughed. "No. I'm Rip Logan."

She looked relieved. "Chloe Keay."

He held out his hand to shake. Her hand was small, two would have fit into one of his, and he was right. Smooth and soft. "Pleased to meet you." He was reluctant to let go. "Are you sure you don't want a ride home?"

She frowned. "Thanks for the offer, but I've called a cab."

"I suppose it's wise. You shouldn't trust someone you've just met."

She looked taken aback and then nodded. "Y–Yes," she stuttered. "Safety first."

As the taxi pulled into the parking lot, Rip's phone rang. He tipped it out of his pocket and looked at the screen. Work.

"Look, I've got to run." He pulled out a card. "Here's my number. Call me Monday morning, and I'll make arrangements to get your car back to you." He handed her the card. "Nice meeting you," he said with a smile and then dashed across the parking lot.

Chloe took the card and watched him go. Coming or going, he was hot.

She climbed into the back seat of the taxi and grimaced at the starting fee on the meter. Safety was going to put a dent in her bank account.

She flipped his card over and read it.

*Staff Sergeant Rip Logan. Ontario Provincial Police, Tactics and Rescue Unit.*

A police officer. Brave and built.

But a risk-taker. How did she feel about that?

One thing was certain though. She could've accepted the ride.

# Chapter 4

On Sunday afternoon, Chloe stood in the lobby of her apartment building and checked her watch. Cory wasn't late—she was early.

She shifted the bags sitting at her feet and wondered again if she'd brought enough. All of her siblings and the three grandchildren would be at her parents' potluck birthday lunch. Pamela had assigned the drinks to her, so she bought two bottles of wine, two-dozen juice boxes, and a case of cream soda.

She usually brought appetizers to family shindigs. Last year, she'd made two kinds of wraps cut into pinwheel finger sandwiches. Chocolate and banana, the kids had devoured those, and gherkin pickle and peanut butter. Delicious. At least, she'd thought so. Pamela had wrinkled her nose and this year told her to bring drinks.

Specifically, wine, juice boxes, and soda. Jeez. Like she didn't know what drinks meant.

Obviously a message in there somewhere. A little jealous, perhaps? Trying to be the favorite aunt? Chloe smiled. It would take more than chocolate and banana for Pamela to get to favorite aunt status. Although, she was handy in a medical emergency. Being cool as a cucumber worked great then.

Chloe waved as Cory pulled up in his Toyota Celica. She had breathed a sigh of relief when he'd offered to drive. It saved answering a bunch of questions about her car.

Her dad considered each of the vintage cars his babies. He lovingly spent hours restoring them. He didn't begrudge them being used. In fact, he prided himself on keeping them roadworthy and made a ceremony of handing over the keys as a gift when each of them turned twenty-one. But she knew, better than any of her siblings, that it stung a bit when one of the cars landed in a shop for bodywork. He fretted.

She picked up the bags as Cory jumped out of the car and opened the door to her apartment building.

"Hi, sis," he said with a smile. He held the door with one hand and reached for the case of soda with the other.

"Hi, Cor. Thanks," she said, handing it over.

"Got drinks this year, did ya? Pam mad at you?"

Chloe laughed. "Served the kids chocolate appetizers last year, and that's all they ate."

Cory nodded. "That'll do it. She gave me something safe, too. The cake. 'Course, she ordered it. All I had to do was pick it up and pay for it." He set the drinks carefully around the cake box in the trunk.

"Make one tiny little mistake . . ." Chloe laughed.

"I know," he agreed, shaking his head.

They settled into the car and fastened their seatbelts. As Cory pulled out, Chloe looked around. "Your car is so clean. It always looks brand new."

He glanced over briefly. "Hard not to with Dad coming over to tinker every few days."

"Do you mind?"

"Heck, no. He's mostly out in the garage with his head under the hood. He doesn't expect me to keep him company. And I don't mind the run out to get him. It's a quick ten-minute drive."

"I know he loves it," Chloe said. "And I think Mom likes the break, too. It's not easy when they have such a confined space compared to what they had before."

"Yeah. And my neighbor's retired and into cars, so he comes over and shoots the breeze with Dad. All in all, it's working out."

"Until Janet decides she wants more privacy," Chloe said tongue-in-cheek.

"Not an issue yet," Cory said with a smile.

"She's not bugging you to settle down and have kids?"

"No." He smirked. "Mom is."

"Of course."

"But Janet and I are fine with the way things are. She's busy with some interior design courses. Maybe once she's done." He shrugged. "One thing at a time."

Chloe nodded. "I'm heading out to the farmhouse on Thursday to start painting. You all done the plumbing there?"

"Yeah. Finished the big stuff Friday morning and passed the inspection. They started drywalling, but I figured I'd wait and install the toilets and sinks once you're done with the painting."

"Thanks. That'll make it easier."

"That's what I thought. I've always got your back, sis."

They turned into the long driveway of the retirement home. Colorful gardens flanked the entrance of the building, and an elderly couple sat on a bench outside the front door enjoying the sunny weather. Cory spotted Dale's car and parked beside it.

"Can you manage?" Cory asked as he lifted the bags. "You take the cake, and I'll carry the drinks for you."

"Are you sure? Pam won't like it."

"That's why we should do it," he said with a mischievous grin.

"Like old times." They shared a laugh as they walked inside.

Pamela had reserved the private dining room and had livened up the cozy space with helium balloons, streamers, and a bouquet of colorful flowers. A gold tablecloth, covering a large dining table, sparkled as it caught the sunlight streaming in through double doors, open at the back of the room. A variety of dishes were already set out on a smaller table against the wall.

Pamela rushed over as they arrived and looked at them with a frown when she saw Chloe carrying a box. "Cake? Where are the drinks? We don't need two cakes," she said with an exasperated voice.

Cory leaned over and kissed her cheek. "Relax, Pam. I've got the drinks here."

Pamela let out a breath. "Thank goodness. Could you put them in the ice over there?" She pointed to a cooler on the floor in the corner of the room and then turned and looked at Chloe. "The cake can go on the dining table. It's warm enough that we can eat outside."

Chloe carried the cake across the room and looked out the patio doors.

The rest of the crew had already arrived. Some of the adults sat on lawn chairs watching the kids toss a Frisbee. Others sat at a picnic table in the center of a stone patio. Bright green sweet potato vine, contrasting with pink and purple petunias, cascaded over the edge of square planters at the corners of the patio.

Ben, Dale's oldest child and an energetic eight years old, spotted Chloe and raced over to grab her hand. "Aunt Chloe," he said as he tugged. "We need you to play with us."

Chloe laughed and followed him outside. She gave a quick hug to her mom and dad and waved at the shouts of hello from the adults as she joined the children playing on the open field.

They played Monkey in the Middle with a Frisbee. Chloe partnered with Ava, April and Scott's four-year-old daughter.

Ava looked up at Chloe with adoring eyes. "I'm a monkey," she said, as she slipped her hand into Chloe's.

"You are a monkey." Chloe smiled and tapped Ava on the nose. "A very cute one."

They played until Pamela called out that the meal was ready. The children raced inside, with the adults trailing behind.

"Did you bring chocolate and banana rolls again?" Ben asked Chloe, as he peered at the food on the table.

Chloe smiled. "Not this time. But Uncle Cory brought a big cake."

"Yippee," cheered Ben. The other kids skipped over to the dining table to take a look.

"For later," Pamela said sternly, shooing them away. "Grab a plate and fill it up. We have chicken, two salads, and veggies and dip. Help yourself."

Ben made a face at the veggies and dip, and Chloe turned away to hide her smile. "Make sure you save room for cake," she whispered to Ben, when Pamela moved out of earshot.

They carried their plates outside to the picnic table. The sun was warm, and the smell of lavender from a nearby garden filled the air.

Chloe sat beside April and then scooted over when Ava squeezed between them. Scott followed and set a plate of food down in front of Ava.

"Thanks, hon," April said as she tucked a napkin under Ava's chin.

"Hey, Chloe," Scott said. "Good to see you. Seems like forever."

"I know. Ava's getting so big." She smiled down at Ava. "And she's eating carrots now."

"No, I'm not," Ava said. "Daddy put them on my plate, but I'm not eating them."

"Don't you want to try them? Ben's eating his," Chloe said, nodding toward Ben, who dipped a carrot stick and then bit into it with a crunch.

Ava watched and then picked up her carrot and poked it into the dip on her plate. She eyed it doubtfully and took a bite. She chewed for a moment and then held it out to Chloe. "You can have it."

Chloe laughed and took it from her. "Thank you." Chloe popped it in her mouth before April could object.

Ava smiled at her. "Aunt Chloe, when can I see Taryn again?"

Chloe swallowed. "Oh, I don't know, pumpkin. It's been a while, hasn't it?"

"Yes. I want to show her my new doll."

"She'd love that." Chloe kissed the top of her head. "Let me work something out with your mom. I'm going to take Taryn to visit her daddy on Friday, but maybe the following week we could come and visit you."

"Is her daddy still in jail?"

"Yes, he is."

"So she doesn't get to see him very often?" She moved the chicken away from the potato salad on her plate.

"That's right. But I go with her every couple of weeks so she can spend some time with him." Chloe wiped her mouth with a napkin.

Ava looked from her mom to Chloe. "How come her mommy doesn't take her?"

Chloe paused. "Her mommy doesn't live near here. Taryn lives with her grandma, and her grandma doesn't drive, so I help out."

Ava leaned closer. "I wish I could live with Grandma," she whispered. "She lets me eat ice cream for dinner."

Chloe chuckled and wrapped an arm around Ava's shoulders. "Grandmas are special."

Ava picked up the chicken drumstick and sat munching while Chloe caught up with all the family news. Dale and Natalie were busy with baseball for Ben and Joey. April was up for a promotion, which would mean longer hours. They were trying to decide if Scott should start working from home to be with Ava. Ava was all for playing with Daddy. April was less sure that the housework would get done. Devon and his partner, Adrian, were thinking of moving to a smaller town outside of Rivermede, and the biggest news of all, Pamela was pregnant.

Fourteen weeks along. Chloe almost choked on her cream soda. She hadn't seen that coming. Last she'd heard Pamela and Rod were having a rocky go of it.

She jumped up and crowded around Pamela with her siblings to hug her. "Congratulations, Pam. How exciting. How are you feeling?"

"Good. The worst of the morning sickness has passed."

"Fourteen weeks already." Chloe did some mental math. Three-and-a-half months. May. How did she keep it secret for so long?

Before she had a chance to ask, Cory walked up. "Chloe, can you listen to this voicemail? Someone left a birthday message for Mom and Dad, but I can't place the voice." He played the message.

"That's Bob Baxter, Mom and Dad's old neighbor."

"Oh, of course. I don't know how you do that. I couldn't figure it out."

"How can you have such an ear for voices and never get song lyrics right?" Devon asked.

Chloe wrinkled her nose. "I can tell you who's singing."

"But not what they're singing," Devon teased.

"Sometimes it's better not to know," she said with a grin.

They gathered around their parents as Pamela carried the cake outside. Dale, in his baritone voice, led them in singing 'Happy Birthday.' Seven candles, one for each decade, flickered in the breeze, and the grandchildren leaned in to help blow them out.

Joy, Chloe's mom, cut and served the cake while Chloe's dad, Hank, opened the cards.

"I bought you a '67 Pontiac Firebird," Cory said when a lottery ticket floated out of the first envelope.

Joy groaned, but Hank grinned. "Thank you, son. I'd love to get my hands on one of those."

Dale and Natalie's card was next. "We bought you a cruise to Hawaii," Dale said with a wide smile.

"Something we both can enjoy," Chloe's mom said as her husband waved the lottery ticket hidden inside the card.

Hank unwrapped Devon and Adrian's gift and held up a toothpaste box. "Toothpaste. Just what we need. Feels kind of light, though." He opened one end and pulled out a folded lottery ticket.

"We bought you a week at a cottage in Sandy Hollow," Devon said. "Fishing, swimming, and all your meals included."

"Perfect holiday. Thank you," Hank said and set the lottery ticket on the pile with the others.

As Joy opened Pamela's card and pulled out the lottery ticket, Pamela said, "I bought you a new set of reclining chairs. And they'll fit in the corner of your living room."

Her mom's eyes shone. "That would be lovely. I can picture sitting there to read."

Pamela nodded and smiled.

Ava came and stood at her grandpa's side as he picked up a pink envelope. "That one's from us," she said.

"Is it now?" He tucked Ava under his arm and held her close.

She helped him open the envelope and pull out the lottery ticket tucked inside. "We bought you ice cream. Lots and lots of ice cream. Enough for a whole year." Ava grinned up at him.

"Marvelous. And we can share it with you," he said, and kissed her upturned cheek. "Thank you."

Ava beamed.

"Last card," Hank said as he picked up the envelope. He opened it up, and leaned over to share it with his wife. As they laughed at the message, Chloe piped up. "I bought you a limousine ride along the waterfront every Sunday with a stop for a picnic lunch. Happy Birthday."

Her parents raised shining eyes as they held the lottery ticket.

"One of these days we're going to win, and all of these wishes will come true," Hank said. "We've stored up a lot of luck over the years."

"But it's never going to be better than spending the day with all of my little chicks together," Joy added. "That's the best gift of all. Thank you for this wonderful party."

Chloe walked over to give her parents a hug. They did have a lot of luck stored up. But what was that saying? Lucky at love, unlucky at lotteries. That probably explained why her parents were coming up to their fiftieth wedding anniversary and hadn't yet cashed in on any birthday lottery wishes.

She, on the other hand, should buy an extra ticket. After the fiasco with Roger, she was due for a lottery win. And then she thought of Rip . . . Hmmm, maybe she'd hold off for just a bit.

# Chapter 5

On Monday morning, Chloe unlocked the back door of an empty storefront property. She locked the door again behind her and walked the length of the space to set her satchel down against the wall of windows at the front.

She moved to the middle of the room, and hands on her hips, eyed the walls critically. It looked pretty good. The pale orange on two of the walls was uneven in patches and needed a second coat. And she'd have to go over the buttery yellow wall one more time to add some durability. But hopefully, a third coat wouldn't be necessary or she'd be staying late.

The owners, three ultra-chic business savvy women, expected delivery of glass cabinets in the morning and had a carpenter lined up for the day after. It was moving quickly, but in ten days they hoped to open their trendy clothing and jewelry boutique. They mentioned they might drop by at the end of the day to see how it all looked.

By noon, Chloe had the yellow wall painted. She stepped back and took a look. Much better. Damn, she did a good job.

She hammered the lid back onto the paint can. There wasn't much paint left, but it would come in handy later for touch-ups.

She stood, arched her back, and stretched her arms over her head. Time for a break. She pulled her lunch out of her satchel, flipped a bucket over, and sat down.

As she dipped carrot sticks in hummus, she wondered how they were coming along with the windshield repair.

How hard was it to replace one of those babies? It looked pretty simple. Pop one out. Pop one in. And most of the popping out was done on Friday night. Half their job was already done. She should ask for a discount.

She crunched an apple and scrolled through the contacts on her phone. Rip Logan. When she'd added his name, she put a little squiggle beside it. A little sperm for her number one sperm donor.

She pressed his number and listened to it ring.

"Rip Logan."

Chloe's heart skipped a beat at his sexy voice. Hopefully there was a gene for that. "Hi, it's Chloe."

"Chloe. Perfect timing. I just got off the phone with Smitty. There's a bit of a snag."

Snag? Pop one in. Pop one out. What's to snag?

"It turns out they can get a new windshield."

"Okay." She drew the word out. They repaired windshields. Wasn't that a given?

"But it's going to take five days."

"Five days? That long?" Her heart sank. "Thursday I start a job at a farm forty-five minutes out of town. I'll need my car. They can't get it done any sooner?"

"Sorry about that. Smitty had trouble finding a replacement."

"Windshields aren't standard sizes?" she asked.

"Unfortunately not. But he did find one that'll fit your Camaro. They're shipping it out, and he'll have it by Friday."

Friday.

"Can you push back the start date for the job?" Rip asked.

"Not really. It's a tight schedule." If she couldn't make it happen, they'd hire someone else. She needed the money, and she wanted the job.

"What about renting a car?"

Bit of a budget stretch, but it was better than losing the job. "Possibly." She wondered if Cory had work out that way. She could hit him up for a ride. Would it be worth it? The questions, the teasing, the risk of her dad finding out? She sighed.

"You know what?" Rip said, interrupting her thoughts. "I think Smitty has a loaner car. I could arrange to borrow it and drive it out to your place tonight. Would that work?"

"Really? Could you?"

"Sure. Give me your address. Actually, would you like to go out for dinner? We could head to O'Malley's for burgers."

Chloe blinked. Yes, yes, and yes. "That would be lovely."

"Perfect. I can pick you up."

Chloe's mind raced. She needed to get the painting done and meet with the owners. If she finished early, she could go home, shower, and change, but in a pinch she could go directly to the restaurant. "Ah, I'm already downtown. I could meet you there."

"Sounds great. Six o'clock?"

"Works for me. See you then." She hung up the phone.

That worked out well. Dinner, a car, and plenty of time to put together a list of questions for her potential sperm donor.

At ten after six, Chloe pulled open the door of O'Malley's and stepped inside. Only ten minutes late. Not bad, considering.

She had finished the painting and had been cleaning up when Serena, one of the owners, had shown up to take a look. Serena was scary perfect. Porcelain white skin, green eyes that matched her intricately knotted scarf, and groomed eyebrows. Pencil-thin and arched as if she always had a question on her mind. It must be spooky waking up beside her at night. Still got a question for ya, bwahaha. Chloe added that to the list—check the eyebrows.

Luckily, scary-eyebrows Serena had loved the colors and wrote Chloe a check. It was always nice to get paid on time, certainly made life easier.

Chloe had power-walked to her apartment and changed into a loose pale blue top over a short black skirt. Then she had strolled back downtown (no point starting the evening off sweaty), enjoying the warm evening.

She tucked a strand of hair behind her ear, with the bangles at her wrist clinking together, and looked around the restaurant for Rip.

He waved when he saw her, and she made her way to the booth at the back. As she approached, he stood up to greet her. Lovely manners and yes, very attractive eyebrows framing those melt-in-your-mouth chocolate brown eyes.

Chloe smiled, and they sat down across from each other. "Hi. Sorry I'm late."

"Not at all." He looked her in the eye. "It was worth the wait."

Chloe's smile widened. "Thank you."

"Would you like a drink? They have some interesting microbrewery beers on tap."

"I've tried Be a Buzz lager," Chloe said. "It's very good, but I think I'll have a lime and soda tonight."

Rip gestured to the waiter and ordered their drinks.

Chloe opened the menu. "Do you know what you're having? I usually have pizza."

"Bacon cheeseburger and sweet potato fries," Rip said.

"You don't have to look at the menu? Must be a favorite."

"House specialty. Can't go wrong."

Chloe closed her menu. "Sounds great. I'll try that, too. Last time I was here, I shared a gluten-free pizza with a friend. It was good, but there's nothing like real dough. It's nice not to have to worry about food allergies."

"Yeah. I imagine eating out would be a nightmare."

No food allergies. Check. "You're a police officer? It was on your card."

"Yeah. I'm with the TRU team. The OPP Tactics and Rescue Unit."

"Sounds like it's more than handing out speeding tickets and directing traffic."

Rip gave a short laugh. "I have done that, but it's been a few years. The TRU team gets involved in high-risk calls. Hostage situations, finding missing persons, executing arrest warrants, that kind of thing."

"Like the SWAT team you see on TV?" Chloe asked, sitting up straight.

Rip smiled. "The Canadian version of it, yes."

"Holy moly. Isn't that dangerous?"

"Can be." He shrugged. "But we lower the risk as much as we can. I work with a great team. That helps."

The waiter interrupted them to serve the drinks and take their orders. When he left, Chloe sipped her soda. The TRU team. Sounded like something a mother would worry about. "Do police officers run in your family?"

"They do. My dad retired after thirty-five years of service, and my sister's a cop up north."

Yikes. "Doesn't your mom worry?" Chloe asked, her brow wrinkling.

Rip smiled. "If she does, she doesn't let on. She's pretty cool with it all. Supports us, loves us despite it." Chloe heard the warm affection in his tone. Loves his momma. Check.

"How about you?" Rip asked. "What's taking you out to a farm this week?"

"I'm a painter. A house painter," she added quickly, hoping to avoid the usual 'I'm not an artist' conversation that followed on the heels of that.

"That would explain the smear of orange paint . . ." he said and trailed a finger down the back of her forearm.

Chloe tingled from head to toe with the light stroke. She cleared her throat. "Yes. I was painting a new store today"—she pointed to the streak on her skin—"this orange color. I must have missed a spot when I washed up."

"Very pretty," Rip murmured.

They broke eye contact when the waiter served their plates. Melted cheese ran down the sides of a toasted bun. The smell of bacon and fresh barbecued beef filled the air.

Chloe draped a napkin across her lap and popped a sweet potato fry in her mouth. "Delicious," she said, tasting the mix of sweet and salty flavors. She swallowed a mouthful and wiped her chin with the napkin. "So, what do you think of the extended warranty plans they sell with electronics?"

Rip shook his head. "Waste of money."

Very good.

"Do you like bagpipe music?"

Rip took a bite of his hamburger and swallowed. "Sure."

Chloe's heart sank.

"It's right up there with cat screeching, nails on a chalkboard, and baby wailing."

Chloe grinned. Two for two. She picked up her burger. "Do you use coupons?"

"What are coupons?"

Chloe looked at the laughter in his eyes and swallowed her mouthful. "You can save a lot of money with coupons," she said seriously.

"I'd rather work an extra shift."

There were worse things. "Do you like to dance?"

"Horizontal or vertical?"

She rolled her eyes. "Vertical."

"Sure 'cause it often leads to horizontal." He took a swig of beer, his eyes never leaving her face.

Chloe's mouth went dry, and she sipped her drink. "Would you consider donating to a sperm bank?" She was curious about why he had done it.

Rip's eyes became guarded. He wiped his mouth and sat back. "I might."

She nodded, feigning nonchalance. "Very altruistic."

"Hmmm. Or if I lost a bet with the team."

"That could happen?" Chloe said with a laugh.

"They have a warped sense of humor."

"Not your ordinary group of friends?"

"Definitely not. Nothing ordinary about them."

Chloe leaned back, stuffed, as Rip finished off his fries. Nothing ordinary about you either, she thought. Dark intelligent eyes that held a bit of mystery. Fiercely loyal, you could hear it in his voice. And strong, if the muscles under the black T-shirt or rippling in his arms were any indication. He was a fine specimen. His sperm were probably competitive swimmers.

If this was a real date, she'd be disappointed if he didn't call her again. But she couldn't imagine she was his usual type. Sophisticated, elegant, smart. She could see that. More like scary-eyebrows Serena. She could see them as a couple. And he'd be brave enough to handle the scary eyebrows in the middle of the night.

But this wasn't a real date. "Thanks for bringing the car."

Rip finished his beer. "No problem. Smitty's going to give me a call on Friday when the windshield's done, so I can let you know."

"Perfect. It's okay if I keep the car until then?"

Rip nodded. "It's all arranged." He pulled the keys from his pocket. "Here you go."

Chloe hesitated. "You'll need a ride home. Can I give you a lift?"

"If it's not out of your way, you could drop me off at the station."

"You brought me a car. It's not out of my way."

They sat back so the waiter could remove their plates. "Would you like coffee or dessert?" he asked.

Chloe looked at the dessert menu. "I'd love a cappuccino." She looked at Rip. "Would you split a fudge brownie with me?"

"What's a meal without a fudge brownie?" he said with a grin.

He was definitely her number one sperm donor.

# Chapter 6

Chloe sat behind the wheel of the blue Mazda Miata and grinned. The car was a zippy little convertible with easy controls, and if she took the corners a wee bit too fast, Rip's body leaned into hers and sent shivers down her spine. She shifted gears and slowed down to turn more sedately at the entrance to the police headquarters.

"Are you sure you don't want me to drive you home? It's no problem," she said, brushing hair from her eyes.

He glanced over. "Thanks for the offer, but I have a bit of work to do tonight."

She pulled up to the main doors. "Thanks again for organizing the loaner. It's a life-, well actually, a job-saver, for me."

"Happy to do it." He stepped from the car and shut the door. "Drive carefully. I'll be in touch."

Chloe grinned. Sweetest words ever. "Thanks. I'll look forward to it." She waved to Rip and drove off.


Rip watched her go and wondered what the hell she was up to. He'd put two and two together and realized she was behind his latest friend request. It was odd that she hadn't mentioned it and odder still that she'd showed up at the game. That, the random questions all evening, some a little too personal, along with posing as a blond, raised a few red flags.

He had run through the possibilities with the current and past list of suspects they had taken down, and so far he hadn't been able to make a connection. But it had him wondering and a bit on edge. She was a sexy little spark plug who radiated innocence, which just didn't jibe.

He pulled open the front door of the police station and swiped his way into the TRU offices. He walked past his own office and headed to the monitoring room.

Two men dressed in office blues sat shooting the breeze, their eyes never leaving the monitors. The younger of the two, Matt Cheeseborough, nicknamed Ched, was the newest member of the team. He sat with his feet firmly planted on the ground, his shirt crisp and pressed, rhythmically tossing sunflower seeds in his mouth and spitting the shells into a bowl at his side.

Experience sat in the other chair. Ed Frenlan, Frenzy to the team, had wrinkles on his brow that matched the wrinkles on his shirt. He leaned back in his chair, his feet propped up on the desk. When Rip walked in, he glanced up briefly. "Hey Ripper, we got your girlfriend on the screen," he said with a smirk.

Rip had reluctantly organized a GPS tracker for the Miata. His Miata. Smitty didn't have a loaner, but Rip used the set-up to get the go-ahead for the tracker. He'd feel like an idiot if nothing came down, but he figured he'd feel like a bigger idiot if he ignored the warning in his gut. Didn't make it any easier with the guys, though. "Tracking my girlfriend. Guess you never had that problem, eh Frenzy?"

"Nope," Frenzy said with a grin. "Was born married."

"You gotta do it," Ched said as he cracked another shell. "Course it'd be easier if you avoided social media altogether. Put yourself out there, put yourself at risk," he said, giving Rip a pointed look.

"You sound like my mother," Rip said. "I'll tell you what I tell her. Loosen up. Live a little."

Frenzy snorted. "Yup. That's what I tell the women-folk too. Loosen up. Live a little. Goes over real well."

Ched grinned and Rip shook his head with a wry smile. He nodded to the screen. "Anything unusual?"

"Nope. Looks like she stopped at a convenience store, but now she's headed to her apartment building. Nothing suspicious."

Frenzy's chair squeaked as he leaned further back. "What do you think she's part of?" he asked in a serious tone.

Rip stared at the screen and watched the red blip move steadily across with slow monotony. "I don't know. Worst case scenario she's part of the drug cartel in Plantation. Maybe with the grow-op doing reconnaissance. Somebody's girlfriend, sister, daughter. It's a wide net."

"Not your average date?"

Rip shook his head slowly. He pictured Chloe and his body stirred. Definitely not average. He wished, but his gut said no. "I think she's after something. I just don't know what."

"We'll figure it out," Ched said with confidence. "We'll break her down. Your gut instinct is golden, and the judge who signed off on the warrant agreed with you. Something's in the air."

Rip nodded. "Feels that way. I'll be in my office doing paperwork for a bit, and then I'm heading home. Text me if anything shows up."

"Will do," Frenzy said with a wave.

Rip headed back to his office and sat down at his desk. Technically, he was finished his shift and could head home. But late in the evening like this, when the offices were quiet, he got the most done. Plus, working odd hours was part of the norm. The TRU team worked when they were needed, twenty-four seven.

He shuffled a few files sitting on the large wooden surface of his desk, and then pulled one over and started reading through it, making comments as he went. He plowed through three-quarters of it, but when the need for another hit of caffeine washed over him, he glanced at the clock and decided it was time to go home.

No calls from the boys. No activity.

Interesting. Well, they'd see. They knew patience. At some point she'd make a mistake. Criminals always did. His job and that of the TRU team was to capitalize on that and come up with an action plan. A main plan, an immediate plan, a backup plan—eventually they'd lay it all out. Yeah, they knew patience, and they'd figure out just what she was up to.

# Chapter 7

The next morning, Chloe zipped around the corner and pulled into the parking lot in front of the convenience store, stopping with a jerk. Man that was fun. The car felt light as a feather and hugged the road. She shut off the engine and stroked the steering wheel. "I'll be right back. Don't go anywhere," she said to the car.

She pushed open the door to the store and walked in with a bounce in her step.

"Chloe," greeted the woman behind the counter, her smile widening. She had masses of gray curls and wore a bright pink shirt. She was a proud breast cancer survivor. "Look at that big grin on your face. And was that a fancy blue car I saw you pull up in? Are you driving here now?"

Chloe laughed. "I know, Bea, it's terrible. It's only a block away, but my car's in the shop, and I was given this loaner to use. It's so sweet to drive, I couldn't help it."

Bea shook her head. "Life's short, sweetheart. You gotta do what makes you happy. I thought for a minute you finally won the lottery."

"Feels like I did, Bea. But this goes back in a week."

Bea printed off a lottery ticket. "Well, here you go, your usual, in the hopes of winning something more permanent," she said as she handed it over. "I'd have mixed feelings if you won. I'd miss your sunny visits in here to buy lottery tickets."

"Aw." Chloe reached across to give her a hug. "Even if I won, I'd still visit you. Better yet, I'll share the money and visit you in some place exotic."

"Now there's a perfect plan," Bea said with a wink. "May you be blessed with lottery luck."

"Thank you," Chloe said, waving the ticket in the air. "And could you throw in some getting-to-work-on-time serendipity, too?"

"You don't need it. You've got a fancy car. But I'll throw in don't-get-a-speeding-ticket best wishes."

Chloe chuckled and threw Bea a kiss.

Potentially, the drive to the job was a quick ten minutes, but with the top down and a few left turns, she could double the sunshine and smooth handling. Chloe turned up the radio, trying not to be distracted by the stream of song titles on the dashboard console. That was something they didn't have back in the seventies. Her car could definitely use an upgrade.

She tapped her thumbs on the steering wheel and sang along to the music. "It's all about the hips, about the hips, no trouble."

Chloe stopped at a red light and watched the title scroll across the screen. 'All About that Bass' by Meghan Trainor. Chloe frowned. All about the bass? Wasn't it all about the hips?

The light turned green and she picked up speed, then slowed again when she spotted the large Weed 'n Feed sign across the top of a warehouse set back from the road.

Wow. The building was massive. This was supposed to be an easy one-day job. She pulled over and checked the address again. Yup. That's the place. She pulled the car closer to the front door and parked.

Chloe put the roof up, grabbed her satchel off the passenger seat, and locked the car. She had her copy of the contract, which had been signed electronically.

This was the first job she had nailed down on her own. Up until then, Margo MacMillan had been in charge of the whole shebang—finding the jobs, speaking with the clients, buying the paint and supplies, and handling all the accounting.

Margo, along with her friend and fellow brainiac, Mikaela Finn, had started the business to help pay tuition in university. Four years of university and more for medical school drained the bank account pretty quickly. Or so she was told. And Mikaela, Dr. Finn now, didn't stop there. She was in the second year of an obstetrics and gynecology residency. Babies, boobs, and female parts below the waist. Good for her.

Margo hadn't been so sure about sticking with the whole doctor circus world. Hard to believe, it seemed pretty sweet. But in the end, Margo sucked it up and dove back in. Family medicine, she had decided. She was in for a hectic two years until her training was done.

In the meantime, Chloe was boss. Well, not completely, but more than she had been. It felt pretty good to be handed the reins. She liked the boss hat. And it was excellent training for the whole mommy role. Chief chef and bottle washer. Bum wiper, burp assistant, social coordinator—she'd be juggling a few hats, and this was primo practice for it.

So getting the contract for this job felt good. One more feather in her cap, so to speak.

The Weed 'n Feed owners had emailed her the dimensions of the space they wanted painted. She had done the calculations for the estimate and faxed the paperwork back for an electronic signature. She hadn't actually made the trip out to take a look. But really, if they couldn't measure four walls, how could they possibly run a business?

She shrugged. Maybe they stored the fertilizer and lawn care products in the warehouse. Having enough room for everything would certainly be a bonus.

Chloe pulled open the door to the store, admiring the weed logo on the glass panel. As she walked in, she was struck by a faint odor. Was that skunk?

A tall, skinny man with a scruffy beard and thinning brown ponytail approached her. "Hello, and welcome," he said, extending his hand.

"Hi, I'm Chloe Keay. I'm here to do the painting," she said, glancing around. The shelves and two large freezers were filled with food. Where were the bags of fertilizer?

"Chris Bellantine." He shook her hand gently and let go. "It's actually a storage area that needs painting. I'll show you."

He led the way through the store to the back. As they walked past the shelves, Chloe spotted some brownies for sale. Odd for a fertilizer store, but they looked quite tasty. Maybe she'd try one at lunch.

Chris stopped in a hallway. There were heavy metal doors to the left and right, and sliding double doors, covered in opaque glass, in front of them. Chris opened the door on the left and walked in, snapping the lights on as he went. Chloe eyeballed the room and thought the four hundred square foot estimate was in the right ballpark. It wasn't a huge space and the fourth wall had a large tinted window in the center. Chloe had a glimpse of greenery through the glass before Chris pressed a button and a privacy screen blocked the view.

"Were those plants?" she asked with surprise.

"Yes. Mostly weed."

"Weeds? Someone needs to get busy," Chloe said with a laugh. "Or do you test your products here? Like a lab?"

Chris rubbed his beard. "Yes, everything is tested here."

"I guess it's the one time having weeds would be handy."

"Uh, yeah. Look, we don't need anything fancy in here. One coat of paint would be good. It's going to be our overflow area."

Chloe ran her hand across the wall. "I'll have to prime it first, but I brought primer and paint with me." She looked around the room. "You wanted a plain beige color?

"White, beige." He shrugged. "Doesn't matter. Do you need a hand carrying anything in?"

"No, I can get it. Should I bring it through the store?"

"If you park on the right side of the building, there's a door across from this one that opens to the outside. You can back your car up."

"Perfect." She nodded briskly. "I'll get started."

Chloe drove the car around and carried in the totes, paint, and a small step stool. She spread drop sheets to cover the floor. It was polished concrete, and storage area or not, it would look better without paint spatters all over it. The primer went on smoothly, and by noon it was done. She decided to stop for lunch to give it a chance to dry before the paint went up.

Just enough time for a chocolate brownie. She grabbed her wallet and wandered out to the store.

There wasn't anyone behind the counter. "Hello?" she shouted into the silence.

She peered between the shelves and then noticed the 'Be back in half hour' sign on the front door. She poked her head into the hallway again to see if anyone was around, but it was quiet.

She shrugged. Surely they wouldn't mind if she took a brownie and left the money on the counter. A sale was a sale after all.

The small square looked scrumptious with its dark chocolate and shiny smooth icing.

Chloe picked one and looked at the price on the bottom. "Six dollars?" She checked the front of the shelf to see if the price was marked there. Nope. Just the sticker on the bottom. "That's outrageous. That can't be right." She flipped another one over. "Six dollars." She shook her head. The thing was tiny. No wonder the store was so quiet. No one could afford six dollars for a brownie. Good heavens. She set it back down and backed out quickly. Thank goodness they were out to lunch. It would have been awkward asking for one and then not buying it.

Wow. Talk about inflated prices. They could benefit from some financial guru advice. A little price and demand workshop. Maybe she should suggest they listen to *Money Market News*. Heck, her parents could give them a pointer or two.

Chloe tossed her wallet back in her satchel. That was annoying. Now she'd be craving chocolate all afternoon. Jeez. Six dollars. Maybe when they came back she could try to weasel an employee discount.

She opened the can of beige paint and got back to work. Halfway through the third wall, she heard voices in the hallway and glanced at her watch. A little longer than half an hour. They could tack on a lesson about tardiness, too.

She set her brush down. Six dollars. Let's just see about that. She strode toward the door.

"Fifty grams."

Chloe stopped short at the edge in the male voice coming from the hallway.

"Fifty grams? We won't be able to hide that. It's too big of a skim."

Chris. She recognized that voice. But gone was the easy, laid-back drawl of this morning. Now she heard anxiety with a tinge of fear. Her heart rate kicked up a notch.

"Not my problem. Should have thought of that before you started this deal. Fifty grams."

"Look. Let me give you twenty now and the rest in two weeks. We can spread it out, bury it in the paperwork," Chris pleaded.

The other man gave a short laugh. Chloe pictured dark eyes and scary tattoos. She stood absolutely still.

"I can take fifty grams of weed or fifty grams of your face. You choose."

Silence. Chloe hoped they couldn't hear the pounding of her heart. Choose the weeds, buddy, choose the weeds.

"All right. All right. We'll do it your way. Fifty grams," Chris said finally.

Chloe released the breath she was holding.

"It's in the back," Chris said.

She heard the swish of the sliding door and the footsteps move out of the hallway.

Her shoulders sagged in relief as butterflies settled in her stomach. Drama in a weed and feed store? What? Maybe Creepy Guy was unhappy with the six-dollar brownies, too. And it sounded like Chris had to think about his choice. His face or weeds? Really? What was the dilemma?

Chloe heard the swoosh of the sliding door again and skipped quietly over to hide behind the door.

"Nice doing business with ya," Creepy Guy drawled from the hallway.

The door to the outside slammed and footsteps retreated behind the sliding door. She wondered if Chris had an office in the back of the building with the weeds.

Chloe picked up the brush to finish the painting and straightened with a start.

Weeds. Weed. Oh my God. Weed.

This wasn't a fertilizer store. This was a marijuana store. Those plants were weed. And those brownies were probably spiked. Holy cow. Still not worth six dollars, but not your average baked goods. What did she walk into?

Either way, she needed to get the job done and skedaddle. The last thing she wanted was for Creepy Guy, or Chris, for that matter, to know she'd overheard them.

She finished painting the last wall in record time and stepped back to take a look. Luckily with the primer, the beige looked great after one coat.

She wrapped the brushes to wash at home, tossed the foam roller in a garbage bag, and scooped up the tarps covering the floor. She rolled them into a ball and stuffed them in the tote bag. The hallway was quiet, so she tiptoed across with her arms full and balanced the load to pull the door open. It took two quick trips to stow everything in the car.

On her way out, she glanced one more time at the store, but Chris hadn't returned.

Normally she preferred to get paid right away when the job was done. But this time, she'd make an exception and slip an invoice in the mail. Hopefully he'd pay it without a problem. It was certainly a better deal than his brownies.

# Chapter 8

Chloe drove straight home with only a minor detour to a bakery to buy a brownie. One dollar and seventy-five cents, thank you very much.

She carried everything inside, cleaned the brushes, and repacked the totes. A place for everything and everything in its place. She sat down at her computer to catch up on her social media while she enjoyed the brownie with a cup of tea.

There had been quite a bit of activity since she'd last signed on. Rip had another baseball game on Friday night, and lo and behold, Jared Clayton had an invitation to a wine and cheese party. Tomorrow evening at a local wine bar, and it looked like he planned on attending. She made a note of the details in her calendar and shut down her computer.

It had been a full day and she was ready for a bath and bed. Painting wasn't usually so exciting. She had tomorrow off and could sort out what to wear to a wine and cheese party, maybe run a few errands in the peppy little convertible, buy the paint and supplies for the job at the farm on Thursday, and sleep in.

She yawned as she ran the bath. That would be a very good question to add to the list for her sperm donors. Up at dawn or snuggle 'til noon?

Good thing she was taking this slowly. There were a lot of important issues to consider.

Rip picked up the phone on the first ring. "Logan."

"You were right, Ripper."

"Of course I was, Ched. What about?" He leaned back in his chair.

"The detectives scanning the GPS on your girlfriend said she spent the whole day yesterday at the weed grow-op out at Weed 'n Feed."

"Really?" Rip said with a frown, sitting up straight.

"Yup. And," Ched drew it out, "you'll never guess who dropped by while she was there."

Rip paused. "Juan Giuseppe," he said slowly.

"Got it in one. None other."

Rip shook his head. "Shit. Anything else?" He picked up a pen and made a note.

"Nope."

"Why would she be hanging out with Giuseppe and Underbelly? Have they found any connection between them?"

"No," Ched said, surprise in his voice. "They can't find anything on her. She's squeaky clean. Not even a parking ticket."

That was exactly how she came across. She was good.

"I guess we sit on it for now. They're pretty close to getting the warrant for Giuseppe. When that happens, we'll get the tapes on him."

"They're talking about adding extra surveillance on her."

"Figure out how deep she's in."

"Yeah."

Rip tapped his pen. "Not a bad idea, especially if the leads dry up. She hasn't made contact with me again, so I guess we wait and see what happens. Let them know I'm available if they need me, and thanks for the update."

"Of course. I'll pass it along."

Rip disconnected the call and tossed his pen down. He leaned back, crossing his arms in front of his chest. It didn't fit. Giuseppe was scum. Chloe Keay was either an incredibly good actress or in over her head. Or both. He'd like to know. He could ask her out again, and he had a pretty good feeling she'd say yes. It might be worth it to see what he could find out.

Yeah, he told himself, it was purely to gather intel. It had nothing to do with the hot body. Images of her flashed through his head. He'd always been a breast man and she definitely caught his attention.

He picked up the phone. Maybe the detectives needed a hand.

# Chapter 9

Chloe tied her hair back in a low ponytail. She'd considered leaving it down, but the night was warm for August and tying her hair back would keep her cool. She checked her appearance in the mirror one last time. The little sundress with its soft material swirled around her thighs as she twirled to look at the back. It really was the perfect length, and she loved the pale pink flowers.

She added another layer of lip-gloss and then tucked the tube inside her purse and snapped the pink clutch shut. All set.

The wine bar was an easy walk downtown, but really, she had a convertible at her disposal. There'd be drinking, obviously, it was a wine and cheese party. But she could ask for a soda and no one would be the wiser. She slipped her feet into sparkling silver flats, grabbed the keys, and locked the door behind her.

The sun was soft this time of night and drew people out for a walk. Farther into the downtown core, the patios were full, and laughter and the clink of glasses spilled into the street.

Chloe pulled into a parking spot half a block from Wine and Chemistry and walked the rest of the way.

As Chloe stepped inside, a young woman wearing a black skirt and a white blouse greeted her. "Hello, are you here for the medical school wine and cheese?"

Chloe tried to hide her surprise. "I am."

"Right this way."

Medical school? Jared's profile said chemistry major. Did he have super-smart doctor genes? Good job, Jared.

She was led to the back and out through a door to a patio. A sleek glass bar hugged the wall and uplights hidden in potted plants added a romantic glow. Groups of people stood chatting, and a low murmur with the occasional burst of laughter filled the air.

Chloe looked around for Jared, but didn't see anyone remotely matching the photos on his page, so she made her way to the bar for a drink.

A glass of fizzy water in her hand, she meandered around the room listening to snippets of conversation.

"It took us half an hour to get that Hazmat suit on."

"I can't imagine. The N95 mask fitting was enough for me."

". . . three cases of syphilis this week. What goes around, comes around."

". . . the best gelato in Italy and the best beer in Prague. I wonder if Charles University accepts transfers."

Look at all the beautiful people in here, Chloe thought. Add smart and well traveled, the gene pool was a bit intimidating.

She spotted Jared when he walked in alone. His profile picture was a good likeness. He waved to a group off to the left and then headed over to the bar. Chloe moved so that he would have to bump into her on his way from the bar to his friends.

Sure enough, drink in hand, he headed her way. She shifted and bam, introductions were made. Interest flared in his eyes (filling out a low cut dress was good for some things).

"So what year are you in?" Chloe took a sip of her drink and watched him over the rim of her glass. Nice straight teeth. Gorgeous thick brown hair. No male pattern baldness issues there. She squinted. Did he pluck his eyebrows?

"Second year of clerkship. Just started," he said, leaning closer.

Oh, slightly nasal voice. Strike one. "It must keep you busy."

"Very. But you know, you learn to balance it all. What year did you say you were in?"

Chloe cleared her throat. "I'm in a lower year. Have you decided what specialty you'll be doing?" she asked, quickly changing the subject.

Jared nodded. "I've decided on interventional radiology."

Radiology. Fancy word for x-rays, she remembered from Margo. Margo had considered that, but hadn't wanted to spend all her time in the dark. Like something nocturnal. Hmmm. She didn't want a baby that was part bat. She wrinkled her nose. Try to stay positive, she told herself. "How many years does that take?"

"About five. They do a lot more now with the technical component linked to radiology. And since it's all digital, you can read films anywhere. It's really exploding as the technology becomes more sophisticated."

Chloe nodded as if she understood what he was saying. Extra bonus points for the big brain. Medical degrees ran in families, didn't they? She'd like to start a branch from that tree. "Do you have time for other stuff? Like playing bagpipes?"

Jared laughed. "No bagpipes, but I do play electric guitar in a band. We don't have any regular gigs, but try to get together and jam."

Musical, check. No bagpipes, check.

"Wow, I'd love to hear you sometime. Any food allergies?"

Jared's eyebrows rose and he stared at her. "Nope."

Chloe nodded and took a sip. Maybe that was too blunt. She'd better ease into the next one. "Have you done your pediatrics rotation?"

"Six weeks in the winter."

"I've heard that's a good one. Working with all those babies."

"Yeah. It was good. Call was pretty light so that was a bonus."

"Oh yeah, definitely. You know I've heard that some people use a sperm bank to have babies. What are your thoughts about sperm banks?"

Jared's eyes narrowed. "I don't think I'll be needing a sperm bank," he said slowly.

Chloe forced a laugh. "Of course not. But you'd consider donating to one, right? There are lots of good reasons to donate. For instance . . ." she trailed off and looked at him.

His eyes shifted from her to a spot in the distance and back again. "Look, it was nice meeting you, what did you say your name was?"

"Chloe."

"Nice meeting you, Chloe. I see some friends over there I'd like to say hello to. Maybe I'll see you around at the hospital."

She sincerely hoped not. "Oh yes, one other thing," she said, touching his arm. "Do you buy the extended warranty for electronics?"

Jared's eyebrows drew together, and he stared at her. "Always." He gave her a tight smile and walked away.

Chloe watched him go. He filled out a suit nicely. He was a lean one, though, and had small feet. More like a bird. But overall, promising. Very smart, nocturnal, musical. She took another sip. He was like an owl, really. More like an owl than a bat. That was good. She could live with an owl.

Well, it seemed her work was done. She hadn't found out why he'd donated sperm, but she doubted she'd get any more information tonight. Apparently talking about sperm made him jittery.

She finished the last of her drink and walked over to set her glass on the edge of the bar.

"Chloe, what are you doing here?"

Chloe turned with a wide smile. "Hi, Margo. Fancy meeting you here." She gave her a hug. And looked up into the smiling pale blue eyes of the man standing beside her. "Trace, you look handsome tonight." They made a striking couple. Margo in a sapphire lace dress with her curls pinned up and Trace with his chiseled features, blond hair, and perfectly fitted suit.

Trace kissed Chloe's cheek in greeting. "I'll get us some drinks. Chloe, can I get you something?"

"I'm just heading out, so I'm fine. Thanks, though."

Trace turned to Margo. "White wine?"

Margo nodded. "Yes, please."

When Trace walked away, Margo turned to Chloe. "This is a pleasant surprise. I thought this was booked for a private medical school function, to give the students a chance to talk to residents in different specialties."

Chloe grinned. "Perhaps. I needed to talk to a medical student about something special so I thought I'd drop by."

Margo's eyebrows drew together. "Really?"

"Yes. Do you remember me talking about having a baby?"

"You're having a baby?" A few heads turned at her raised voice.

"Well, not yet," Chloe said, glancing over to see Jared staring at her. She lowered her voice. "I'm still choosing my sperm donor. It's not something you want to rush."

"No. I imagine not," Margo said dryly.

"I've narrowed it down and the handsome, and I might add, very smart, Jared Clayton is one of my top two." She turned and waved her fingers at Jared, who looked a little pale.

Margo followed her gaze. "Does he know that?"

"No. I had a few questions for him before I make my final decision." She leaned closer. "I didn't want to raise his hopes and then not choose his sperm."

"Yeah, I imagine that would be devastating," Margo said, tongue-in-cheek. "He already looks a bit freaked out."

Trace returned with the wine and handed a glass to Margo. "Did you come out to enjoy the wine and cheese, Chloe?"

"Nope. I was here to interview my potential sperm donor."

Trace smiled broadly. "You can never be too careful."

Chloe waved her hands. "Exactly. That's exactly what I've been saying."

Trace nodded and took a sip of wine, laughter in his eyes as he caught Margo's exasperated expression.

"You're not supposed to have access to their names, I thought?" Margo asked.

"I'm ahead of my time," Chloe said smugly.

Margo nodded with a smile. "Speaking of which, how'd it go on Tuesday? I was looking at the schedule to fit in a job, and I saw you finished early."

"Yes, it wasn't quite what I expected." No need to burden Margo with all the pesky details. "It looked great after primer and one coat, so it was quick."

"Good. I have a repaint job for one of the Bennett homes. I'll add it in."

"Can do. I start the job at the farm tomorrow, but after that there are one or two free days."

"That would work. The timing would be perfect, actually." Margo sipped her drink.

"I should probably head out," Chloe said. "Tomorrow starts bright and early, and I should get my beauty sleep." She leaned over to hug Margo. "You have a great evening." She kissed Trace on the cheek. "Good luck sorting out your future. There's a lot of positive energy in this room. You're lucky to be a part of it."

"I am. Thanks, Chloe. Do you need a cab?"

"Not tonight. I have a car." With a small wave, she turned to go.


As Chloe unlocked the car door, she heard her name called. She turned and watched as Jared jogged up to her.

"It's Chloe, right?"

"Yes."

He gave her a quizzical look. "Have we met before?"

"About fifteen minutes ago."

He grimaced. "Yes, I remember that. I meant before tonight."

Chloe shook her head. "No, I don't think so."

His shoulders relaxed. "Okay, then. I thought I overheard your friend say you were pregnant and wondered if I should be worried."

Chloe smiled. "I think we'd have a beautiful baby together, but I'm not quite ready for that yet."

He laughed, relieved. "Me either." He tilted his head. "I'm sure a night with you would be unforgettable . . ."

Chloe's smile broadened.

". . . I don't know why I was so worried."

"You like to keep track of your sperm?"

He stared, his eyebrows drawn together. "What?"

Was he blushing? Chloe laughed and brushed her hand on his chest. For a guy who donated to a sperm bank, he was a bit shy. "Look, I should get going. I have an early day tomorrow."

Jared took a step back. "Of course. Sorry to keep you," he said, distracted.

"Not at all. I really enjoyed meeting you." She turned to go and then stopped and looked back. "Do you prefer M&M's or Skittles?"

"I don't really like chocolate, so Skittles?"

Chloe nodded and gave a little wave good-bye. "Toot-a-loo." She sat and swiveled to swing her legs into the car. No point in giving a peep show. Jared stood watching her as she pulled out of the parking spot and eased into traffic.

Doesn't like chocolate? What? What kind of human being doesn't like chocolate? Wow – strike two. Maybe that was his problem. He really needed to loosen up and enjoy a bit of sugar. She drove along, her mind reeling. About halfway home, she slowed. On the other hand, if a child didn't like chocolate, it could really work in the parent's favor. After all, someone would have to take care of the Easter Bunny treats. Think of the money she'd save, the Halloween chocolate she'd get to eat. She nodded, considering. Maybe that was a plus. A big plus. More chocolate for her. That sounded like a good thing.

Chloe let herself into her apartment building and pressed the button for the elevator.

Now that she'd met both Jared and Rip, she was going to have to make a decision. Her appointment was coming up in two weeks. How to choose?

She unlocked her apartment door and stepped inside. She slipped off her shoes and set her purse on the table. It was a warm night and the breeze through the sliding door to the balcony drew her over. Pushing the door open wider, she went outside and leaned against the railing. Six floors below, lights from the street lamps shimmered, and she watched a couple strolling hand in hand.

Jared or Rip?

Either way she couldn't go wrong. They were both prime. But who would be the heir and who the spare?

Jared had his good qualities. Big brain, musical talent, chocolate-hater (good thing she put that into perspective), small feet. His only drawback was the slightly nasal voice. Not so apparent out on the street, though. Maybe the ambience had some effect on that. And her parents would be so proud to have a doctor in the family.

And what about Rip? Her heart skipped a beat. A little bit of testosterone heaven. The Rip-spawn would kill spiders for her. Definitely a protector. Nice deep voice, a tad tall, but athletic, fun to be with, lived in the moment (no need for that extended warranty), and shared dessert. Didn't have to worry about any germ phobia, there. And he loved his momma. Oh, she forgot to ask Jared about that. Jared was a bit skittish. Did she want a skittish baby? But he was a doctor. She could live with a skittish medical progeny. She could make that sacrifice.

Overall though, if she had to choose between sharing chocolate or eating it all herself, she'd probably prefer . . . to eat it all herself.

Yeah, that's it. It looked like Jared's sperm would be the heir and Rip's the spare.

She sighed and a feeling of contentment washed over her. Nice to have that decision out of the way. When she went to work on Saturday, she'd fill out the paperwork and set the sperm aside. She could get this baby rolling.

The street was quiet with only a rustle in the trees as the breeze picked up. Time for bed. She had an early start tomorrow.

Jared watched Chloe drive away.

What did she say? 'You like to keep track of your sperm?' That was an odd comment.

He grunted and headed back toward Wine and Chemistry. Granted, most of her questions were odd. M&M or Skittles? Extended warranty? Food allergies? Weird.

He'd almost shit his pants when she looked at him across the room and used the word baby. There was no way he wanted to end up like Robbie, paying paternity to a one-night stand for the rest of his life. He'd heard about scams like that, and it was worse now that he was in medicine. Of course, Robbie called him paranoid, but he'd rather be paranoid than write checks for a child he didn't want.

And his father would kill him. Jerome Gerald Clayton was running for office, and if Jared did anything to embarrass him or smear the family name, Jared was pretty sure he'd come after him. Not that his father had a history of violence, but there was a lot invested in the election. His dad had advisors, campaign managers, and a street team who had been working full-time for the past year to put the platform together. Luckily, Jared was peripheral because school took priority, but if he did anything to screw it up, the shit would hit the fan.

He pulled open the door to Wine and Chemistry and headed back to the patio. His heart rate was finally slowing, and he could use another glass of wine. That was a close call.

# Chapter 10

At eight o'clock the next morning, Chloe put the top down on the convertible and settled inside. The farm was a good forty-five minutes out of town, and she was going to enjoy every one of them.

She had tucked her hair up under a ball cap to keep it from flying everywhere, and with the liberal use of sunscreen, she was ready to enjoy the open air. Could they make her Camaro into a convertible? It was so sweet. Maybe she could drive around without a windshield. At least until winter.

She maneuvered out of the downtown core and turned onto the country road. Normally, out on the back roads, she'd open it up and speed, not excessively mind you, just enough to get there on time. But today she cruised at the speed limit and enjoyed the sunshine and fresh breeze.

At eight thirty on the dot, Chloe pulled into the driveway of the farmhouse. The main house was a large two-story building, with a welcoming wraparound porch, set back from the road. There were little touches like a pot of bright flowers on the step and colorful cushions on the chairs of the porch. Obviously someone had an artistic flare and cared for their home.

The driveway curved around to the back, so Chloe followed it and parked in front of a barn, which showed signs of the recent renovation. The barn's old siding had been replaced with red brick to match the house. Black shutters graced new windows and elegant carriage lanterns flanked an impressive glass and wooden door.

Chloe hooked the strap of one of the tote bags on her shoulder and made her way over to the barn door. It stood ajar and she heard hammering inside, so she knocked and walked in without waiting for an answer.

Wow. When she became old and gray, she wanted a granny suite like this. One more reason why big-bucks Jared spawn was a good idea.

It had been converted into a bungalow with an open plan kitchen and dining area across the back wall and a sitting room to the right. They'd left the high ceilings and added windows to let the light stream in.

She set the tote down and followed the sound of the hammering down a hallway to the left, past a large bathroom (she'd have to go back and take a closer look later), to the bedroom.

A man wearing overalls, with a rim of red hair poking out from under a baseball cap, backed out of the closet as she walked in.

"Hi, I'm Chloe Keay. I'm here to do the painting."

"Pleased to meet you, Chloe. Dennis." He extended his hand in greeting. "We were expecting you. I think it's all ready to go. I've got a few finishing touches to do, like getting these shelves up, but I can stay out of your way."

Chloe smiled. "Looks like there's plenty of room for both of us. I can get started in the kitchen and dining room."

Dennis nodded. "I hope you don't need me to tell you the paint colors 'cause I've got no idea about that."

Chloe waved away his concerns. "No worries. I've got it all sorted out."

"Good. If you need a hand, just shout."

"Will do. Thanks." She paused at the door. "Actually, would it be okay if I borrowed your ladder?"

"Absolutely. Help yourself."

Chloe made her way back to the car as the hammering started up again. She carried in what she needed and started the process of prepping the walls. It was all brand new drywall so she wiped the dust off and made sure it was smooth. She could use a combo paint and primer product, but Margo was old school and always used plain primer first, so Chloe followed suit.

She worked her way around the three walls of the kitchen and dining room, and started on the sitting area, happily listening to tunes through her ear buds.

"That's a boring color."

Chloe started at the female voice and turned, pulling the ear bud from her ear. "Oh, you startled me," she said pressing a hand to her racing heart.

A tiny woman wearing a loud purple tracksuit and matching purple sneakers stood in the front doorway with her hands on her hips. "Maybe if you weren't wrecking your hearing with those plugs, you wouldn't be so jumpy." Her silver curls bounced as she walked over to the kitchen.

Chloe pulled out the other ear bud. "Perhaps not."

"White? Really? You got no sense of style?"

Chloe laughed. "I don't pick 'em. I just put 'em on the wall."

The woman grunted.

"Actually, this is the primer. The color for the kitchen is a pale yellow. I can show you." Chloe walked over and pulled a color fan out of the tote. She shuffled through it and stopped at a yellow sample. "This is what it'll look like." She held it down so the woman could see.

The woman stepped closer and peered at it. "It's all right, I suppose. Better'n white. What's going up in there?" she asked, pointing to the sitting area.

Chloe flipped through the fan and stopped at a pale mauve. "Brazen Lady," she read with a smile.

The woman's face split with a grin. "Really? Even if I didn't like the color, I like the name. What else you got?"

"Boring white for the bathroom and Orgasm Peach for the bedroom."

The woman snorted. "There's no way my uptight daughter-in-law would pick Orgasm Peach for the bedroom." She chuckled and looked at Chloe with a twinkle in her eye. "Good one."

Chloe smiled back and tucked the fan back into her tote. "You must be Ruby McGee."

"I am."

"I'm Chloe. Nice digs."

Ruby looked around, nodding. "Yeah. But don't tell them I said so. When they told me I was moving into the barn, I wasn't too happy. I thought I'd be out here between the cows and the cats. But it cleaned up real good. I'm kinda looking forward to it now."

Chloe picked up her roller and dipped it in the tray of primer. "Where you moving from?"

"I have, well had, a house in Merrickville. A cute little back split. I've been living there for darn near my whole life. Married, had kids, watched them grow up and have kids of their own. I figured I'd die there, too. But I made one little mistake with the oven and wham bam, I'm told I'm moving closer so they can keep an eye on me. Orgasm Peach," she said with a chuckle. "I like that." She wandered closer to Chloe. "Do you want a hand with that?"

Chloe hid her surprise. 'No' sprang automatically to her lips, but when she looked over, she saw the proud tilt of Ruby's head and the hopeful question in her eyes. "Have you painted before?"

"Did all my own decorating at one time or another."

She handed Ruby the roller. "Don't fall off the stool. I'm not sure we have insurance for that."

Ruby took the roller and laughed. "I promise not to sue." She dipped the roller in the tray, blotted off the excess, and rolled the primer on the wall in smooth even strokes. "I can cover the bottom six feet for you anyway. Trouble with being short."

"Short? Think of it as the fun size, like those little chocolate bars." Chloe set up the ladder to reach the top edge close to the ceiling. "When is all this supposed to be finished?"

"They told me another two weeks. Painting, the last of the plumbing, and a bit of carpentry is all that's left. My stuff's been in storage for the past month 'cause my house sold a lot quicker than they thought it would. A week Saturday they'll move it all in here."

"It'll be nice to get settled. The painting should be done by the middle of next week, maybe sooner with the extra help."

Ruby worked at a steady rhythm rolling the primer on the bottom half of the wall. Chloe finished the edging and then followed behind Ruby covering the top half of the ten-foot high walls.

"Lot of height for a short person. I'll have to find some tall friends to fill it," Ruby commented as she painted.

Chloe laughed. "Do you know many people in this area?"

"A few. I've visited often enough to have met some of the other farmers and their families. They're a real social bunch, especially in the winter. I often head over to the Preston farm. Merv and Millie started up a little restaurant, a bistro they call it."

"Sounds fancy."

"It's not bad. They use produce from their farm." She shrugged. "I guess it's a way to keep the income up in the winter. Even though Millie's my age," she said shaking her head. "It seems to be the thing to do these days. Find a second career, at age seventy." She dipped the roller in the tray. "Don't know that I'd want to start up a restaurant, but I must say, this painting's nice. Gets me off my butt," she said with a grin.

"Let's hope your muscles don't complain too loudly tomorrow."

"I'll be fine. I like to be active. And useful."

"I appreciate the help."

"If we finish early, maybe you could take me for a spin in your car? And put the top down? That's one sexy set of wheels." She turned and waved the roller. "I should get me one of those. And a driver to drive it. Somebody tall." She grinned at Chloe with a twinkle in her eye. "Got to live up to my Orgasm Peach walls."

# Chapter 11

Later that evening, Chloe let herself into her apartment and tossed the keys on the table by the door.

She pulled her T-shirt over her head as she walked to the bedroom. She shimmied out of her shorts and pulled out fresh clothes. Bundling her hair up off her nape, she padded to the kitchen.

On her way through the living room, she pulled open the sliding door. It was warm out, but the breeze was cool. Thank goodness for her east-facing apartment. The west ones must be sweltering this time of day.

Dinner. What she wouldn't do for pizza, even leftover pizza. She opened the refrigerator. No such luck. A tuna wrap it was.

She chopped a red pepper, sliced an avocado, and added diced tomato and onion. As she mixed in the dressing, the phone rang.

Chloe put it under her ear and continued to stir. "Talk to me, babe."

There was a pause. "Hi, Chloe."

Her heart skipped a beat as she recognized the voice. "Hey there, Rip. How's it goin'?" She transferred the phone to her hand and set down the spoon.

"Great. How are things with you?"

"Wonderful. I started painting at the farm today and Smitty's Miata is a dream to drive. I'm going to have to arrange a windshield repair more often."

Her heart swirled at his deep chuckle.

"This should work out well then," he said. "Smitty called and said the windshield arrived and they could install it tomorrow. But, could you wait until Sunday to get your car back?"

"It'd be a sacrifice," she said, tongue-in-cheek. "But I think I could manage. Seriously though, they don't need the Miata back sooner?"

"No, it's fine. I'm going out on a call, probably for the next forty-eight hours, but I wondered if you'd like to go to a baseball game on Sunday? The Tangs and Falcons are playing. I could get tickets and drive your car out when I pick you up."

"I'd love that. I haven't been to a Tangs game in years." She was nine and it was decidedly boring. Somehow she didn't think it'd be boring with Rip. "Sounds like fun."

"Perfect. I'll come by your house at about twelve thirty. That work for you?"

"Yes. I'll be ready. Thanks, Rip."

"My pleasure. See you Sunday."

She hung up and finished making her tuna wrap. Two more days of the zippy little convertible and plans to see Rip. Sounded like the perfect weekend.


Friday night after work, Chloe pulled up to the curb in front of a small apartment building and shut off the engine. The late afternoon sun was warm, but she left the top up on the convertible. She was picking up Taryn and she didn't want the four-year-old flying out of the car if they hit a bump. Hmmm. She'd probably have to rethink the whole convertible thing once she had small fry around. Kids and the top down probably didn't go together.

She locked the car and tucked the keys in the pocket of the capris she wore.

There were six units in the building. Three of the apartment doors, painted a dingy yellow, faced the front and opened onto the sidewalk. The other three, including Taryn's grandmother's, were at the back.

Chloe walked around the building. The old brown siding on the walls had faded over time and was showing signs of wear, but a small patch of green lawn was neatly kept. A row of bright orange marigolds and purple pansies grew against the building.

Chloe stepped up to the middle door and knocked.

"She's here." She could hear Taryn's excited voice before the door opened.

"Chloe," Taryn squealed and wrapped her arms around Chloe's legs.

Chloe bent, rubbed Taryn's back, and hugged her. "Hi, Taryn."

Taryn's grandmother made her way slowly down the hall, lurching to the left with each step. "Hi Chloe," she said with a warm smile.

"Helen." Chloe walked closer and gave her a hug. "You're looking well. Did you shake off that summer cold?"

"Yes. Finally. That was a nasty one, but I'm feeling much better."

"I was admiring your handiwork in the garden. The little flowers are flourishing."

"Despite the less than ideal conditions." She gave a crooked grin. "It's my specialty."

"I'm in charge of watering them," Taryn piped up.

"You're doing a fantastic job. Both of you." She smiled at Helen. "After we visit Derek, I thought Taryn and I could go back to my place for a bite to eat and maybe bake some cookies. I could have her back by eight. Would that be okay?"

Taryn clapped her hands. "Cookies. Yeah."

Helen smiled. "Sounds like the perfect plan." She pulled a small pink jacket out of the closet. "I was thinking about your parents. Don't they celebrate a birthday in August?"

"Celebrated their seventieth birthday last week and had the whole family together. Mom was in her element."

"She'd love that. How are they keeping? I miss them. I don't get out to see them as much anymore."

"They're doing well. You know, Ava was asking if Taryn could visit. Maybe next week we could arrange something. You could visit Mom and Dad, and I could take Taryn to see Ava."

Taryn jumped up and down, and Helen's eyes shone. "That would be lovely. As long as it's no bother."

Chloe shook her head. "Never. I'll check everyone's schedule."

Helen held out the jacket. "Here Taryn, take this with you and come give me a hug."

Taryn raced over and hugged her grandmother. She took the jacket, picked up her backpack, and skipped back over to Chloe. She slipped her hand into Chloe's and looked up.

"Ready?" Chloe asked.

Taryn nodded, her pigtails bobbing.

Chloe took the backpack and waved to Helen as she shut the door.

"I've got a special car today. Wait 'til you see it." She swung Taryn's hand and grinned as Taryn skipped along beside her.


"Do you think Daddy will be happy to see me?" Taryn asked quietly from the passenger seat.

Chloe glanced over. "He always is, honey. Are you looking forward to seeing him?"

"Yes."

Chloe heard the hesitation in her voice. "What did you bring to do today?"

"Cards and checkers. And I brought some crayons to draw him a picture."

"He'll love that, Taryn. Another page for your book."

Taryn looked out the window. "Jackie said Daddy was a bad person. That's why he's in prison."

Chloe's heart ached. "What did you tell her?"

"I told her what you said. He's not bad. He did something big wrong and now has a big timeout."

Chloe nodded. Wrong place, wrong time. Bad decision. Lives destroyed. How do you explain that to a four-year-old, let alone the four-year-old's friend? "And what did she say to that?"

"She said he was still bad," Taryn whispered.

Chloe's lips tightened. Kids could be cruel. "She's never met him Taryn, so she doesn't see the good side of him."

"I love Daddy."

"Of course. It's okay that you love him and that you miss him."

"I really like to see him."

"He really likes it when you visit him, too. And when you finish grade one, he'll be done with jail, and you'll be able to see him more."

"I just have to do grade one and then he'll come home?"

"Yes."

"That's a lot of sleeps."

"It is Taryn," Chloe said softly. "But in the meantime, we can visit him and you can draw him pictures. And we'll make them into a book that he can keep when he gets home."

"Okay. I think I'll draw him a rainbow and put me and him at the end of it."

Chloe smiled. "Together again. He'll love it."


Derek did love it.

After they made their way through the metal detectors and through the bag inspection, they sat together at a small table in a room set aside for families. The room was painted a pale blue, a step up from the dull gray everywhere else. An unsmiling guard stood by the door, and Taryn's father wore a jumpsuit, but the light that shone in Taryn's eyes, and Derek's too, made the trip worthwhile.

Chloe had been coming with Taryn for about a year. Two months after Derek was arrested and sent to jail, Taryn started waking up at night with night terrors, worried that she'd never see her dad again. She became withdrawn at school and already a picky eater, became more so.

Taryn's mother had never really been interested in Taryn from the start. She had flown the coop and as hard as that was, it was probably better that she was out of the picture.

Derek had stepped up to the plate and had filled both parents' shoes. But when he came up with the boneheaded scheme of trying to use someone else's credit card and ended up in the slammer, it was doubly tough for Taryn. She lost both parents in one fell swoop. Luckily, Derek's mom, Helen, was granted sole custody and provided some much needed love and stability.

It was slow going, but Taryn had settled into a routine. She met with a counselor once a week and along with her grandmother, attended family get-togethers once a month with kids and families of incarcerated inmates. They could share their experience, which made it seem normal. Well, as normal as it could be. But the meetings and the visits did have the effect of calming Taryn and reassuring her that her dad was okay.

"Go fish, Daddy," Taryn said.

Derek picked up a card. "Uh-oh, you only have one card left."

"Do you have any threes?"

Derek handed over a card, and Taryn grinned.

"I win." She set down a pair of threes and looked at her dad.

"Again," he said with a smile. "You're getting so good at recognizing all your numbers. I can't beat you anymore."

"I know my letters, too. I could read you a story. I brought one."

"I would love that."

Taryn pulled a book out of her backpack and pushed her chair closer to her dad's. He put his arm around her shoulders, and she opened the book and started to read.

When she turned the last page, Derek swallowed and collected himself. "Holy cow. What a great job you did, Taryn. Super reading."

The guard walked over and tapped Derek on the shoulder.

"You'll have to bring another story when you come again," Derek said. "I think it's time for you to go now."

Taryn jumped down. They collected the crayons and paper, folded the drawing she had made, and packed everything carefully inside her backpack. After tugging the zipper closed, she turned and hugged her dad. "Bye, Daddy."

"Bye, sweetheart. Be good for Grandma."

"I will."

Taryn hitched her backpack onto her shoulders and walked over and tucked her hand into Chloe's.

"Bye, Derek. See you in a couple of weeks."

"Bye, Chloe. Thanks so much for bringing Taryn."

"You're welcome."

Chloe always found this part the hardest. Saying good-bye. Taryn used to get tearful, but with the regular visits, it was much easier. Now she handled it better than the adults.

Chloe and Taryn were buzzed out and taken back through the metal detectors. Their bags were searched again, and they were cleared to go. They walked outside into sunshine, but the sun was low.

Chloe checked her watch. "Five thirty, Taryn. Are you hungry?"

Taryn nodded. "Yes. For sketti."

Chloe hitched the backpack on her shoulder. "Spaghetti, it is. Luckily, I have all the ingredients we need at home."

"Yippee," Taryn shouted and gave a little skip. "I like going to your apartment."

"And we can make chocolate chip cookies for dessert." She had some Pillsbury cookie dough tucked away in her freezer. For some homemade goodness, all they had to do was set the rounds of raw dough out on a cookie sheet and bake them. That little Doughboy was a genius.

Taryn looked up at her with hopeful eyes. "Maybe we should make those first so they're ready when we're done our sketti."

"Excellent plan."

Chloe unlocked the doors, fastened Taryn's seatbelt over her car seat, and headed home.

# Chapter 12

On Saturday morning, Chloe pulled into the parking lot in front of the convenience store. Leaving the car engine running, she dashed inside.

"Thought you weren't going to make it," Bea said to her as she held out a lottery ticket.

Chloe handed her the money and took the ticket. "The draw's tonight. I gotta be in it to win it."

"Good luck. I've got my fingers crossed for you," Bea said with a wave.

"Thanks, Bea." Chloe turned on her heel and rushed back out the door. She hopped in the car and peeled out onto the road.

If she could drag herself out of bed fifteen minutes earlier, she wouldn't have such a mad dash. But really, what was the fun in that? This way she got fifteen extra minutes of sleep. There'd be time to dawdle on the way home.

She pulled into the sperm bank at nine o'clock on the dot. Perfect timing. Leaving the top down—no rain in the forecast any time soon—she headed inside. She went through the usual routine of turning on the lights and computer and adjusting the music in the waiting room. In the kitchen, she plugged in the kettle to make a cup of tea. Bobbing the teabag in the mug of steaming water, she walked back to the reception.

The first appointment wasn't until eleven, which gave her plenty of time to set up her sperm.

She went into the files, ready to fill out the paperwork. Only a week and a half until the big baby-making date. She was getting excited. The more time she spent with Taryn, the more love she felt she had to give. They'd had such a great time together the night before. When Taryn had hugged her good-bye, Chloe's heart had been ready to burst.

So, less than two weeks to go. It was close enough that she could put a hold on 4652 Rip Logan and reserve 2485 Jared Clayton.

She frowned and clicked around. Where was 4652? She scrolled through the file. Wow, he was a popular guy. When she checked three weeks ago, there had been at least two vials. Now there were none. Did she miss a sale? Jeez. Good thing he was the spare. She held her breath until she found 2485 Jared Clayton. Phew, that was close. Still available, three left. Thank goodness. She couldn't imagine starting the whole process again. All that research wasted. She took a sip of tea.

Well, not to worry, it all worked out. She carefully filled out the form, saved it, and printed it off. With the last click and the sample reserved, she threw her arms in the air and twirled around in her chair. A little bambino was on the way. Man, that felt good.

Those financial gurus were right. It was a relief to have a retirement plan in place.


Jared pulled into the sperm bank parking lot and turned off the ignition. His eyes narrowed. That car looked familiar. He sat, frowning, until it dawned on him.

It was her. That's what she'd been driving. What was her name? Carol? Cleo? Chloe? Yes that was it. Chloe.

He stepped out of his car, sweat breaking out on his forehead despite the cool morning air.

How could he forget? Ever since he'd met her, he'd had this nagging worry. Something wasn't quite right.

He went over and over all the crazy questions she'd asked. What was it? Why did it put him on edge? Her comment 'you like to keep track of your sperm' had echoed in his head.

And then the light went on.

He hadn't really thought about his donation to the sperm bank. He'd done it on a lark, really. They had asked university students to donate, and he thought it very altruistic at the time. After all, if it could help someone out, why not?

Okay, here's why not. The laws had changed. He had been okay with donating anonymously, but the possibility that two people could inadvertently end up in an incestuous relationship had started a huge debate about the right to know the identity of the biological parents. The long and the short of it was no more anonymous sperm donation. If a child wanted to know the name of the sperm donor, it would be released. He could understand it. Hell, he agreed with it. He'd want to know, too. Part of his father's election platform was the wholehearted endorsement of the right to know. In fact, Jerome Gerald Clayton wanted to streamline the process and make it even easier.

It would never occur to his dad that their family would be affected by the fallout. God, the press would have a heyday.

It had been on Jared's to-do list to visit the sperm bank and remove his samples. Make a withdrawal at the bank, so to speak. But school got busy and he just forgot. Until that Chloe woman started asking all those bizarre questions. Then it dawned on him that he never did get around to it. It went up the list to 'put out the fire' priority.

He wiped his brow. His biggest fear was that he was too late. He never procrastinated and this was why.

He yanked open the door and strode into the waiting room. He stopped when he saw Chloe sitting behind the counter.

Chloe looked up and her smile widened. "Jared. How are you? Great to see you. Did you come to make another donation? What perfect timing. Your supply is getting low." Chloe reached for a clipboard.

Jared felt nauseous. "How low?"

"Three left. Well, I guess only two now. I chose your sperm for my baby and set it aside. In two weeks, we'll be parents. Hopefully. I feel very fertile, so as long as they're strong swimmers, I don't think there'll be a problem." She beamed at him. "Isn't that exciting?"

"No. It's not exciting. I've changed my mind, and I want all the sperm back. I don't want children this way."

Chloe frowned and sat down. "Really? I did extensive research. You should be very proud that I picked you. There was some stiff competition, so to speak."

He clenched his jaw at the joke. "Well then, you won't have any trouble picking someone else."

"Oh, but I really want you."

Jared stiffened. "I'm sorry, Chloe, but it's not gonna happen."

Chloe's shoulders sagged. "What made you change your mind?"

He tried to ignore the disappointment in her eyes. "I thought about it more, and with all the media attention around sperm donation, I've seen it from a different perspective. I never thought about how the kid might want to know their parent."

"I'd keep it confidential. I promise I won't tell anyone. I can give you back the other samples, it's not a problem. But please reconsider mine. Just think about it, give it twenty-four hours. Please. If you still want it then, I'll return it to you."

"Chloe—"

"Please. I swear, I won't tell a soul where it came from."

Jared looked at his watch. "I have to get to the hospital." He sighed. "Okay, Chloe, twenty-four hours. But if I don't change my mind, I get it back?"

Chloe nodded reluctantly. "Yes." She pulled up the forms she needed. There were forms for this. She filled it out quickly and had Jared sign and then went to get the vials with his sperm.

"Thank you," he said quietly, his hand trembling slightly as she passed them to him.

"You're welcome." She looked at him with unhappy eyes.

Jared turned and strode out of the office. He reached his car and realized he didn't get her number. Hell, he didn't even have her last name. He had no way of contacting her. It was unlikely he would change his mind—this had kept him awake for the last three nights. But she had looked so sad, and he didn't have the heart to deal with it right now. He glanced at his watch again. Shit. He couldn't be late.

He glanced at the convertible. What about her car registration? It'd have her address, and he wouldn't have to go back in. The car was open, the roof down. It'd be worth a look. He walked over, leaned into the car, and flipped open the glove compartment. Sure enough it was right there. He pulled out his phone, took a picture, and then threw the piece of paper back inside the glove box, closing it with a snap. Done. At least he could get in touch, and hopefully by then she'd have come to accept that he wasn't ready to be a father.

# Chapter 13

Chloe pulled on white shorts and a loose orange sleeveless top. It was going to be a scorcher of a day and from what she recalled, baseball games were long. Seriously, she once baked three pies while watching a game on a Sunday afternoon. The pies were out of the oven and cooling and the game was still only three-quarters of the way through. Light clothing and SPF 50 today for sure.

She pulled her hair up into a ponytail and picked orange and pink dangling earrings. A matching bracelet, a light spray of a citrusy perfume, and she was all set.

Rip said he'd be by around noon, so Chloe had a quick snack, brushed her teeth again, and checked that her purse had everything she needed. Cell phone (thank goodness for game apps—a few levels of Save QB! would keep boredom at bay), a travel-size deodorant stick (might need a refresher), Halloween-sized package of Skittles (in case she was peckish), an extra pair of socks (she once stepped in a puddle and had to wear wet socks all day—she learned her lesson), and a wallet-sized CPR instruction card (2 breaths/30 pushes or 3 breaths/40 pushes? She could never remember). Prepared for every contingency, she tucked it all inside the orange and pink handbag and zipped it closed.

At five to twelve, Chloe tied the laces of her running shoes, grabbed her hat and purse, and headed down to wait in the lobby.

Just as she stepped out of the elevator, Rip walked up to the front door. She waved and let him in.

Rip reached down to brush a soft kiss on her cheek, and Chloe caught a musky scent that stayed on her skin when he pulled back. Musky was her new favorite.

His eyes swept down the length of her and her heart skipped a beat at the desire that flared. She felt it, too. That need to touch his skin, the pull between them.

She had a fleeting thought about asking him to donate sperm again. It would save her the trouble of insemination—with the attraction between them, she was pretty sure his sperm could find her eggs across a crowded room.

"You look lovely. Are you a Falcons fan?" he asked.

She looked at the Tangs T-shirt stretched across his muscular chest. Mi casa et su casa. "No, I'm a Tangs fan."

He looked at her quizzically and then smiled. "Okay. Your car is out front. We might as well take the Miata."

"Awesome. I love the convertible."

"Do you want me to park yours around the back?"

"No, I have a spot in the underground garage where the Miata is now, so we can leave my car there. I'll go with you, and we can make the switch."

Rip handed her the keys and held the car door open for her.

Chloe slid in, appreciating the familiar feel of her own car. "Smitty did a great job with the windshield. It looks brand new," she said when Rip sat down in the passenger seat.

"Yeah, it was worth the wait. Luckily, he found one that fit."

"I hope it wasn't too expensive."

He shrugged and glanced over at her with a smile. "That was worth it, too."

Chloe smiled back, her heart fluttering at the look in his eyes.

She drove into the parking garage and pulled up beside the Miata. She dug in her purse for the keys and handed them to Rip.

He backed the Miata out of the parking spot so Chloe could pull in, and by the time she joined him, he had the top down.

When they drove out into the sunshine, they both slipped on sunglasses and a hat. Chloe pulled her ponytail through the back of a baseball cap adorned with a pink and orange swirl, and Rip tugged on a blue Tangs cap.

He glanced over at her as he drove. "You wearing sunscreen? You're so fair, you'll burn in the sun."

Aw. She always wanted a boyfriend who cared about sun protection. It was so sweet. "I am. Sun-proof factor 50. Don't leave home without it," she said with a grin.

It was a forty-minute drive to the stadium on the outskirts of town. Rip parked a couple of blocks away, and they walked the rest of the way. When he reached for her hand, she looked up at him with a smile. Her hand fit perfectly with his. And he was an interlocker, not a clasper. She was pretty sure that said something about equality.

After checking their tickets, they found the gate they needed and climbed a ramp to their section. Their seats were three in from the end of the row, and the three men who had to stand to let them pass were more than a little grumpy. Whoa, what was that all about? Why the hostile glares?

She used deodorant. The game hadn't started. What was their problem?

She sat down, leaning closer to Rip, and looked out at the sea of blue and white. The stadium was almost full and every fan wore the Tangs' colors in some shape or form. T-shirts, caps, jerseys, jackets, even a Tangs cowboy hat. One keen fan wore a Tangs tuque. That poor soul might need to borrow her deodorant in a bit.

The Tangs players jogged out onto the field to warm up, and Chloe clapped along with the others. A couple of players greeted fans at the edge of the field and signed autographs. Pairs practiced catching, four more sat and stretched, and a trio of players ran short sprints. They weren't as pretty as Rip, but they were all right. She'd take their sperm. For others.

A short time later, Chloe watched as the Falcons filled the dugout, and a small group of them filed out onto the field. In their *orange* uniforms. Her eyes widened and she bit her lip as she looked down at her shirt. She couldn't have picked a better match if she tried. Jeez.

She looked over at Rip's laughing eyes. "You don't have a jacket, do you?" she asked.

He squeezed her hand. "We can buy you a T-shirt."

The announcer's voice on the loudspeaker interrupted them. "Good afternoon and welcome to Rivermede Royal Stadium. Please stand for the singing of our national anthem."

The crowd stood en masse, and hats were removed.

Chloe felt a burst of pride as voices from the crowd joined in the singing. Her voice rang out. "O Caaaanada, we stand on cars, and freeze. O Caaanada, we stand on cars, aaaand freeze."

The three men beside them looked over and burst out laughing. Chloe frowned. Her voice wasn't that bad.

Rip tugged her hand, and they sat down as the first pitch was thrown.

The fans clapped and cheered with the plays, and Chloe enjoyed the crescendo of excitement when a ball sailed toward the wall. It would die abruptly if the ball crossed the first or third baseline, but the crowd went wild when one of the Tangs hit it into the stands beyond the second base. One time, after a quick scramble, the jumbotron screen flashed with the image of a young boy sporting a huge grin, his arm in the air, and the ball in his glove.

The cameras panned the crowd and caught couples watching the game intently, babies wearing little blue onesies, and fans with the wildest hats and the craziest dancing.

The wave was the most fun as it swept around the stadium with a roar. Chloe was on her feet with her hands in the air as it passed by.

Rip filled her in on the player statistics (only twenty-two years old and pitching in front of a sold-out crowd, with a what? Ninety-mile-an-hour pitch?). And he bought her a hot dog and a box of Cracker Jack (no talk of risk and high taxes in this ballpark).

Chloe found an excuse to touch Rip's arm, run her hand over the taut muscles of his bicep, press her thigh against the side of his, and lean closer to catch her new favorite musky scent. How did she ever think baseball was boring?

Too soon, the game was over.

Hand in hand, they made their way out of the stadium, stopping to buy her a T-shirt.

"For next time," Rip said.

Chloe grinned and picked one that looked identical to Rip's. She'd seen celebrities do that. Obviously, that's what made their skin look so good—no furrowed brow trying to choose what to wear.


Rip wrapped his arm around Chloe's shoulder and drew her close. She fit perfectly. Her head tucked into his shoulder and her soft curves brushed against his side.

He caught a hint of her sweet scent that reminded him of Florida sunshine.

It crossed his mind to slow it down and take it easy. His heart and head warred a bit on that one. She was still on their radar. They were looking into the connection between her and Derek Sly after her little rendezvous at the penitentiary. That, her visit to Weed 'n Feed, and an excessive number of runs to the mini-mart near her apartment, kept the file open. But after spending the afternoon with her, he highly doubted she was a criminal mastermind. She was too open and too naive to be hanging out with the scum of Rivermede. Unless it was all an act or a damn good con.

Well, one way to find out. Spend more time with her. Funny how his head and heart agreed on that one.

"Would you like to head to O'Malley's for a bite to eat?" he asked. "It's still early."

She glanced up at him with a smile that made him glad he'd asked. "Love to."

With the top down, they drove the forty minutes back and parked in front of O'Malley's.

Rip pulled open the door to the tavern and stepped aside to let Chloe go in first. When Chloe walked in, two men from a group of four sitting off to the right looked over and waved.

"Chloe!" one of them called out.

"What? Chloe's here?" A young man with a mop of red hair and a full beard, swiveled in his chair. "No-o-o-o-o," he said, raising his hands dramatically, his face crumpling.

The dark-haired guy beside him threw back his head in laughter and slapped the redhead on the back. "Kiss it good-bye, mate," he hooted.

The redhead covered his face with his hand and with an exaggerated heave, pretended to sob loudly. "Say it isn't so."

Chloe shook her head at them with an amused smile and followed the waitress to the table beside them. Before they sat down, Chloe turned and introduced Rip to the four men. "Rip, these are the always-hopeful, never-successful, group of Sunday regulars. Pete, Steve, Caleb, and the very sensitive Cam. Guys, this is Rip."

As the others raised their hand in greeting, Cam turned hopeful eyes to Chloe. "Tell me you're not going to play tonight. You're just here for food, right?"

"Oh, I don't know. I'm always up for free pizza," Chloe teased.

Pete laughed loudly. "It's more than a pizza coupon tonight. The winner gets a free weekend getaway in one of Bennett's finest suites."

Chloe's eyes widened. "Wow. What's the occasion?"

"Tim O'Malley's birthday. Bennett Homes tossed him two weekends in their fancy spa suite, and Tim made one of them the prize tonight."

Chloe nodded. "Very nice. I'm going to enjoy that," she said, giving Cam a cheeky look.

Cam groaned. "No-o-o-o. I have to win this for Genie. It's our anniversary tomorrow, and that's the gift."

Chloe waved her finger at him. "Cam, an anniversary gift should come from the heart, with your hard-earned money, so it means something."

Cam looked pained. "I was going to work for it. It would've been hard."

"Well then, maybe I'll play. When you win, you'll have earned it."

"When I win," Cam muttered. He snorted. "Fat chance with you playing."

"What kind of attitude is that? Isn't Genie worth a bit of effort?"

Cam straightened. "Hell ya. Okay, Chloe-ears. I accept your challenge. Bring it on."

Chloe grinned at Cam and sat down in the seat Rip held out for her. She leaned over to Rip and whispered, "He doesn't have a hope in hell."

Rip laughed at the twinkle in her eye. "Sounds like you're a regular here. How come I've never bumped into you?"

"Oh, I mostly come on Sunday nights. Whenever I feel like free pizza." She opened the menu. "Looks like Tim's added some new entrées."

Rip didn't bother checking.

"Aren't you going to look?" she asked.

"No need. It couldn't be better than their bacon cheeseburger and sweet potato fries."

"Tofu and bean sprouts on gluten-free bread," she read from the choices. "That doesn't pique your interest?"

"Some things are just too special. I'll leave it for those who truly appreciate fine dining."

Chloe laughed and closed her menu. "You're right. I'll have the burger and fries, too."

After the waitress took their order, Rip sat back and stretched his legs under the table. "Did you have a busy week?"

Chloe took a sip of water. "Not too bad. I'm out at a farm painting a barn."

"A barn?"

"They're renovating it into an in-law suite. It's one fancy barn. And the granny moving in is a real sweetheart. Actually, she's been helping me paint."

"That doesn't change your routine?"

"No, she's great. I do all the corners and edges, but she covers the rolling. At least, on the bottom six feet where she can reach," Chloe said with a grin.

"She probably loves the company."

"Yes. She talks my ear off, but I don't mind. I used to work with my boss, Margo MacMillan, but she's off pursuing higher education, and I miss the chatter. And Ruby is a bit of a wild woman, so the stories are pretty entertaining." She leaned back as the waitress set plates in front of her and Rip.

"Déjà vu." Chloe smiled as she shook her napkin onto her lap.

Rip leaned forward. "The view is even better the second time around."

Chloe swallowed, a lovely tingle spreading through her. "Did you have a busy week? You said you were on a forty-eight-hour job. Seems like a long shift."

Rip bit into a fry and nodded. "We were called up north. Some guy with a hunting rifle barricaded himself inside an empty cottage. We weren't sure if he had anyone else with him. It took thirty-six hours, but in the end, the guy surrendered peacefully and nobody got hurt."

"Wow, that could have ended badly in so many ways."

"Not if we do our job right," he said with a shrug. "Then there really is only one good outcome." Rip took a bite of his hamburger. "Do you know Juan Giuseppe?" he asked causally, carefully watching Chloe's expression.

She looked at him blankly. "No, I've never heard of him. Should I?"

Rip sighed quietly in relief. Not even a hint of recognition in her eyes. "Not necessarily. I wondered if you'd come across him painting." That much was true.

"Doesn't ring a bell. I'd have to check to see if he was one of our clients, but off the top of my head, I don't remember a dude with that name."

"Are you mostly painting in private homes?" he asked.

Chloe swallowed her mouthful and wiped her lips with a napkin. "Mostly. We do all the painting for Bennett Homes, in any of the buildings he owns. But we have a few commercial accounts too. Earlier this week, I spent a day painting a new store and another day, I was at Weed 'n Feed."

The opening he wanted. "Weed 'n Feed?"

"Yeah. I painted a storage room." She picked up a French fry and waved it at him. "Something's fishy about that place, though." She popped the fry in her mouth and chewed.

Rip raised his eyebrow at her, but sat silently.

"It's not what I expected." She picked up another fry. "I thought they sold lawn care products, you know, weed and feed."

"That makes sense," Rip said to encourage her.

She looked pleased. "Thank you. Well, apparently not." She leaned closer and lowered her voice to a whisper. "I think it's for growing marijuana." She sat back. "And they sell brownies for six dollars."

Rip tried not to laugh at the outrage on her face. "Maybe they're extra special."

Chloe snorted. "No brownie is that special. Six dollars!"

"I would stay away from there," Rip said quietly, watching her closely.

"Amen to that. The place gave me the creeps," she said with a shudder.

Rip nodded and relaxed. They'd need more information from her later, but for now he could leave it.

They finished their hamburgers and were munching on the last of the fries when the bartender picked up a microphone. "Hey there, folks." He waited until the hellos from the crowd died down. "Welcome to the Sunday evening edition of 'He said. She said.' We've got a good one for you with a prize you're going to want. A two-night stay in a luxurious Bennett suite. Don't get that every Sunday." He waved an envelope in the air as Cam and the boys hooted and hollered. "Who wants in?"

Cam's left hand shot in the air. He pointed to Chloe with his right hand, narrowed his eyes at her, and nodded slowly. "You're goin' down," he mouthed at her.

Chloe laughed and put her hand in the air as the bartender came around and handed out earpieces and numbered remotes. Rip took one, too. What the hell.

The bartender made his way around the room until a dozen players were ready to go.

They put the earpieces in, checked for sound, and tested that the remotes recorded their guesses.

"Okay, all set. We've got you all. You can watch the screen to see how you're doing," he said, pointing to the large television mounted on the wall in a corner near the bar. "And here's voice number one."

Rip listened to the snippet of a movie scene through the earpiece. He couldn't say what movie it was from, but the voice was Morgan Freeman. He picked his answer from the multiple choices listed on the screen. After twenty seconds, the bartender closed the responses and the correct answer flashed green.

Not bad. One right.

After five voices, Cam, Chloe, and two others were in the lead with no errors. He managed to get three correct. No fancy, free-weekend hotel package for him.

Chloe was as cool as a cucumber with every question. Listened briefly and with no hesitation, only a serene smile in Cam's direction, punched in her answer.

Cam looked like he was running a marathon. Pete, Steve, and Caleb were his pit crew. As the clip played, Cam extended his arms in the air to demand silence. Pete mopped Cam's brow, and Steve and Caleb screened him from the others so his choice would remain a secret. They whooped, jumped in the air, and high-fived each other with every correct answer.

Down to the last two, Chloe and Cam were neck and neck. Rip silently cheered for Chloe. In between each recording, Chloe carried her end of the conversation with him as if nothing was happening in the background.

To his mind, the voices became more obscure. He hadn't heard of the movies or the actors, but apparently Chloe had. It was impressive.

The last answer was punched in and Chloe turned to Rip. "Is your family in town?"

Rip stared at her. Couldn't she feel the tension in the air? Cam and his crew were completely still, their eyes focused on the screen.

"My sister's up north in Beauregard, and my folks live in Emerson, a small town about an hour away," he said.

Chloe nodded and took a sip of water. "Mine are mostly in town. Two brothers border the outskirts, and two sisters and a brother live in Rivermede."

The bartender wove his way toward them and stood between the two tables. "We've tallied the results, folks. Thank you all for coming out tonight and participating in our special birthday edition of 'He said. She said.' And a huge thanks to Bennett Homes for providing our grand prize tonight—a weekend getaway in their spa suite. It is my pleasure to announce the winner. Congratulations . . .

Chloe." With a flourish, he turned and handed her an envelope.

"Ahhh." Cam collapsed, hung his head, and banged his fist on the bar. "So close," he said through gritted teeth.

"Good effort, mate," Pete said, slapping Cam's shoulder.

"Valiant attempt," added Steve.

"You did the best you could," Caleb said, raising his beer and taking a sip.

Chloe took the envelope. "Thanks very much." She eyed Rip for a moment with a question in her eyes, and he held her gaze. Maybe he'd be getting that weekend in a fancy hotel, after all.

Cam came over to the table and stuck his hand out for Chloe to shake. "Congratulations. I bow to your talent Chloe-ear. I hear the next level of voice-recognition software is going to be based on your brain."

Chloe laughed and instead of shaking, put the envelope in his hand. "Happy Anniversary, Cam. Say hello to Genie for me."

Cam stepped back, his eyes wide. "Really? Really?" He jumped three feet in the air. And then settled. "No, I can't. You won it fair and square. You could use this."

Chloe smiled. "I thought of it." She glanced briefly at Rip and then spoke again to Cam. "But I won it for you. Go and enjoy it with Genie. She'll appreciate the sweat and tears that went into it."

Cam reached down and plucked Chloe out of the chair in a bear hug. He swung her around and with a grin from ear to ear, set her down. "Thanks, Chloe. You're the best."

"You owe me a pizza."

Cam pointed his finger at her. "You got it. Any time." As he walked away, he jumped and clicked his heels in the air, making them laugh.

Rip watched him go. Somebody was going to get lucky. He glanced over at Chloe, who watched Cam join his friends. She smiled broadly, with a look of love, as the four friends high-fived and chest-bumped.

A flash of jealousy caught in his gut. He wanted that. He wanted that kind of look aimed his way.

But it wasn't that easy. Hell, he still had a trace on her car. He looked at Chloe thoughtfully. He could call that off. There was no way this was an act. She couldn't be that good. All his instincts told him she wasn't lying. The likelihood of her being connected to any drug scheme was so remote it was laughable. Which was exactly how the rest of the guys were going to see it. He was going to take a ribbing over this one.

But it still didn't answer the question—why did she show up on social media and at the ballpark? The question still niggled at the back of his mind. What did she want?

He knew what he wanted. He wanted to find out if her skin was as soft as it looked, if he would taste a bit of Florida sunshine on her lips. She fit perfectly against him. She was beautiful, his eyes roamed lower, built, and fun. He loved her laugh and wanted to hear it more.

So, what did she want? He caught the twinkle in her eyes and wondered. Could it be the same thing? Could it be that simple? Was there a chance he'd get lucky, too?

# Chapter 14

The following afternoon, Chloe was at the barn painting the walls in the bedroom, still thinking about her date with Rip. Next time, she might just keep that Bennett suite gift certificate. That would be a deliciously sexy prize to share with Rip. She wasn't sure if he was quite ready for it, but if there was a next time . . .

"Yoohoo, Chloe! Are you there?"

Chloe set down her roller brush. "In here, Ruby."

Light footsteps made their way down the hall and then Ruby poked her head into the bedroom. "Oh good, you're still here. I was worried you'd be finished, packed up, and gone."

"Almost done, except for a few touch-ups. I missed you this morning."

Ruby stepped into the room, onto the tarp covering the floor. "Spent the morning in the doctor's office." She made a face. "My doctor needs more patients. Then he wouldn't want to see me so often."

Chloe laughed. "Your misspent youth is catching up with you."

"You think? I was healthy all through that. Maybe I just need to misspend some more."

"I like the way you think."

Ruby looked at the walls. "It looks really good. I love the color."

"I'm glad. From a barn to a chateau with a few strokes of paint."

Ruby snorted. "And a mere eight million decisions." She turned to Chloe. "I'm sorry you're almost done. I enjoyed helping with the painting."

"I appreciated all your help, too," Chloe said. "You'll have to change it up every year, so I can come back and see how you're doing." She smiled. "Or I could just come visit."

"Sounds like a better plan. Would you like to go out for lunch? My treat on your last day. I thought we could go over to Millie's new restaurant."

Chloe looked over at her with surprise. "Why, that's lovely. Thank you, I'd love to."

Ruby glanced at her watch. "It's eleven thirty now. I'll call and double check they have a table. Never used to need a reservation, but it's gone viral. We tried to go there for dinner a couple of weeks ago and couldn't get in."

"Isn't that a good thing?" Chloe asked.

"I don't know. Maybe. Maybe too much of a good thing." She frowned. "Millie looked like she was run off her feet."

Chloe winked. "Maybe she could use a hand."

Ruby stared. "I like the way you think," she said with a laugh. "I'll have to check that out. I'll go call. Be right back."

Chloe hammered the lid onto the paint can, wrapped the brush to clean later, and started to fold the tarps. She had a few more spots to do in the bathroom and kitchen, but the bedroom was all finished.

With everything packed, she stopped and took one last look around. She really liked this color, too.

She carried the load to the kitchen and set it down as the front door opened.

"Good news. They have a table, but we'd have to leave now. Can you take a break?" Ruby asked.

"Perfect timing. I want to vacuum the bedroom, but I should let the paint dry first. A break now would be great." She brushed a hand down her T-shirt and shorts. "Is it a fancy place? I didn't bring a change of clothes."

Ruby scoffed. "Heck no. It's a farm. You look fine." She fluffed her hair. "We can always tell them we got windblown in the convertible."

"I don't have the convertible anymore."

"They don't need to know that," Ruby said, as she led the way out the door.

Millie's farm was only 'one street over,' but it was far enough that they needed to drive. They settled into Chloe's car with Ruby giving directions. Out the driveway, make a right. Turn left at the rickety fence around the big ditch and slow down when you pass the big boulder.

"If you see a water tower, we've gone too far. There, up on the right." Ruby pointed. "Do you see the sign?"

"That one?" Chloe saw a faded wooden sign that read Presto. "Is that the name of their restaurant? Presto?"

Ruby grinned. "Yup. They were trying to decide on a catchy name, but a news reporter came out to do a piece on it and mistook that old faded sign for the name of the restaurant. And it stuck." She chuckled. "All the out-of-towners come looking for Presto. Millie didn't have the heart to tell 'em that Merv just never got around to fixin' that sign. It used to say Preston Farm."

"Procrastination paid off. Presto's a catchy name."

They turned right and followed the gravel lane lined with trees until it opened into a small parking lot. Chloe pulled up between a beat up pick-up truck and a shiny black sedan.

"Looks like they've got a few customers. Come on, she's expecting us." Ruby led the way under a garden trellis, covered in orange and pale yellow roses, at the edge of a forest of trees.

Chloe stopped and looked around. "Where you taking me, woman?"

"Oh, just a little nature hike to work up an appetite," Ruby said with a chuckle. "Just kidding. This is actually the back of their property. Millie said she didn't want to have a bunch of yahoos walking through her pansies, so she made Merv make a path to the back door. See?"

A newly painted sign with an arrow directed them through the trees.

Ruby marched along the path cushioned with pine needles and lined with pots overflowing with deep purple petunias and bright yellow begonias. "Good thing it's not raining. We'd get wet."

Chloe laughed and skipped to keep up.

The path opened up to a manicured lawn and a panoramic view of the farmhouse, which stopped Chloe in her tracks. "Holy snickerdoodles, Batman. That's not what I expected."

The grand two-story building was pristine white and had a newly renovated addition off the back. The roof extended out to cover an open-air patio. White square pillars with shaker-style panels rose to the ceiling and flared in a decorative curve. Pale green curtains, in a gossamer-thin material, hung straight down on either side of the columns.

Ruby stopped and glanced at Chloe. "Impressive, eh? Wait 'til you taste the brisket." She grabbed Chloe's arm and tugged her toward the entrance.

A short gentleman with a portly belly and cropped hair came out through glass double doors carrying two plates.

Ruby waved. "Merv. Merv, hi."

Merv turned and his smile widened. "Ruby. Good to see you. Let me set these down. I'll be right back." He walked over and set the plates in front of an elderly couple. He chatted with them for a moment and then returned to greet Ruby and Chloe. "Did you come to try the brisket, Ruby?"

"You bet. Can't get enough of it. Is Millie in the kitchen?"

"She is. Gearing up for the lunch crowd. You can go on back and say hello if you like."

"I'll just poke my head in." She turned to Chloe. "This is Chloe, Merv. She's been fixing up the barn for me."

"Nice to meet you, Chloe. Welcome to Presto."

"Thanks." Chloe turned to Ruby. "You go ahead and say hi to Millie. I'll let Merv show me to a table, and I'll sit and enjoy the view."

Ruby headed to the kitchen, and Merv grabbed two menus and led Chloe to an open spot in the corner.

"Ruby's been raving about the food, but she didn't mention how pretty the restaurant is," Chloe said, admiring the tables. Each was covered in a white tablecloth and set with apple green napkins, shiny silverware, and a vase with a single pink Gerber daisy.

Merv pulled out a chair for her. "Folks, especially the city folk, seem to like the fussy. Me, I just want good food. Here's a menu for you."

Chloe took it. "Thanks. I'll look it over, but the brisket comes highly recommended."

"It's a fan favorite for sure," Merv said with a wink. He filled her water glass, and then with a small salute, moved to the next table with four women eating lunch.

Chloe opened the menu to check out the desserts. Be good to know how much room to save.

Apple pie and ice cream. Mmmm. Blueberry strudel and oh, her favorite, chocolate brownies. The brownies had a little green star beside them. Highly recommended, she bet. She glanced at the price.

Six dollars. What? Again? Chloe looked at the other prices. Three dollars for apple pie and blueberry strudel but six dollars for the brownies. What?

Hopefully the brisket was filling.

She set the menu aside and sipped her water as she looked out over the backyard. A chipmunk raced up a tree and three chickadees flittered on the branches at the edge of the forest.

Ruby returned from the kitchen and sat down with a frown.

"What's wrong, Ruby?" Chloe asked.

"Something's up," she said. "I don't know what exactly, but something's up. Millie isn't her usual bubbly self. She looks stressed. She's a farmer's wife. She's never stressed."

"Do you think it's the restaurant? Maybe it was more than she bargained for."

"Maybe." Ruby leaned closer and lowered her voice. "I thought it was going extremely well. Money seems to be flowing from the money tree right into their laps. They've added this addition, painted, repaired the house and the barn. Farming didn't foot the bill for all that. I thought they'd found a gold mine in brisket." She shook her head. "Don't even look at that," she said when Chloe shifted the menu. "You've got to order the brisket."

Chloe smiled and moved the menu to the corner of the table. "Brisket it is."

Ruby leaned back and placed her napkin on her lap. "I've already placed the order."

Chloe finished the last bite of her lunch and wiped her mouth. "You're right, Ruby. Best brisket ever. I'm stuffed."

"I know. I could eat it every day. You want dessert?"

Chloe patted her stomach. "I couldn't fit it in. I think I'd need a siesta if I did this every day." She set her napkin on the table. "I just need to use the loo."

"Inside and down the hall. Second door on the left, just before the living room."

"Thanks, Ruby." Chloe wove her way between the tables, went through the glass double doors, and walked down the hall, admiring the photos hanging on the walls. Four kids, all in graduation caps and gowns, three in wedding photos. Busy household.

As she neared the living room, Chloe heard someone talking.

"Here's the next batch," a male said.

Chloe froze. That voice. She recognized it from Weed 'n Feed.

"Ah, now. You told us it was a one-time thing. For that private party. That's not what we agreed to. The missus isn't too keen to take that on."

*Merv. Why are you talking to Creepy Guy?*

"Well, I think the missus better rethink her plan if she wants to keep this little venture going."

"Now come on, be reasonable. I said we'd try it. We tried it. But it just ain't what we want."

"I think what you want became insignificant when you took the money. That's a hefty loan to pay off selling brisket and chicken."

There was silence. "We'll pay it off."

"Great. Ninety grand by Friday."

"What? We can't get that kind of money together by Friday. You said it was a five-year loan."

*Oh, Merv. What've you gotten yourself into?*

"I did, didn't I? Well, the rules changed. Ninety grand by Friday." He paused. "Unless you want to keep the pot pie and chocolate brownies on your menu. Your choice."

"That's not what we signed on for. And it's seventy grand," Merv said with an edge in his voice.

"Interest," the other voice drawled. "Ninety."

Chloe heard a rustling.

"You're wasting my time. I'll be back on Friday. Keep this." Chloe heard a soft thud. "I'll want lunch when I come. You can let me know what you've decided then." There was a pause. "Oh, and by the way, don't think about going to the police with this. You'll never prove I was involved. And you've been serving pot to the public. That's called trafficking. We'll see you in jail before I ever get there."

Chloe heard footsteps and quickly ducked into the bathroom and shut the door. Her heart racing, she turned on the water and flushed the toilet to make some noise.

She waited a few minutes, and then with shaking hands, opened the door and peered into the hall. Coast clear. She made her way back to the table. Ruby was paying the bill, so Chloe sat quietly and waited until she finished. She debated whether to tell Ruby but maybe the less said the safer.

They got up and made their way across the yard to the car.

"Thank you very much for treating me to lunch," Chloe said to Ruby. "That was delicious."

"Don't mention it. You've worked hard. I'm happy to treat you to something special."

Chloe smiled weakly. She was pretty sure Ruby wasn't aware how special that brisket might be.

# Chapter 15

Chloe waved good-bye to Ruby. "Have fun!" she said with a cheeky smile. Ruby had spent the drive home complaining about having to spend the afternoon with her daughter-in-law, shopping for a new sofa. Chloe suspected she wasn't as put out by it as she pretended.

Ruby snorted as she started across the driveway. "I should drag you along."

"If I didn't have painting to do, I'd be right there with you."

Ruby chuckled. "As if." She stopped and turned. "Keep in touch," she said sternly, pointing her finger at Chloe.

"Of course." Chloe jogged over quickly and gave Ruby a hug. "Enjoy your new space."

Ruby smiled slowly, her eyes misting. "I will. I just won't tell them."

With a wave, Chloe went into the barn and shut the door behind her. She fished her cell phone out of her tote and scrolled through her contacts until she found Rip's number. Hesitating only a moment, she tapped the screen to dial it.

It rang once. "Logan."

"Hi, Rip. It's Chloe." She cleared her throat.

"Chloe. This is an unexpected pleasure."

It really was too bad his sperm weren't available. "I need your help."

"Is it an emergency?" His voice was all business.

"No, no," she said hastily. "I think something might be brewing." She bit her lip. "Actually, it's just a feeling. I may be wasting your time . . ."

"Time with you would never be a waste."

Ah. Her heart melted. "I'd feel better if I could tell you about it in person. Could we meet?"

"Absolutely. Officially at the office or unofficially for dinner?"

Creepy Guy's threats echoed in her head. But hey, food. Stealth won. "Dinner. Some place quiet would be good."

"Are you in danger, Chloe?"

"No. I don't think so, but someone I know might be." She winced as she said it. Even to her it sounded a bit wild.

"Why don't you come to my place? We can talk there and won't be overheard. Eighty-two Mask Road. Say six thirty?"

Chloe sagged in relief and blinked away tears. He believed her. He didn't think she was crazy. "Okay," she whispered.

"Chloe, keep my number handy. If you feel unsafe, call me."

"Thanks, I will. See you soon." She hung up and sat for a moment, relieved to have Rip's broad shoulders on her side.

That voice sounded menacing to her and Merv didn't seem too happy. Merv might not be able to go to the police, but there wasn't anything stopping her. She hoped it was the right thing to do. A picture of Rip's dark eyes and hard body swam in her thoughts. He was making her dinner. How could that be wrong?


Later at home, Chloe scrubbed a paint smear off the back of her arm and stepped out of the shower. She rubbed her skin with a scented lotion that was new. Watermelon Kiwi. She had hesitated buying it, afraid she'd smell like a fruit salad. But when she had dabbed it on her wrist to try, it had a faint musky rose fragrance. Surprisingly pleasant. It wasn't until after that she worried it might smell like a moldy fruit salad. Love me, love my masked pheromones, she thought with a shrug.

It was a warm evening so she chose a mint and cream flowered chiffon skirt, which skimmed her thighs, and a matching pastel green camisole. She pulled her hair up, curled the loose tendrils around her face, and added dangling crystal earrings.

She looked at herself in the mirror. She didn't want Rip too distracted by what she wore. Maybe she should grab a light sweater.

Now, which purse? She considered what she needed to bring. She tapped her chin. Breath mints. Check. Chocolate. Of course. How could you solve a crime without a good quality dark chocolate? Spy goggles and walkie-talkies—hopefully he would provide those. Hmmm. That was probably it. The small jeweled clutch it was.

Strappy sandals and she was ready to go.

She knew exactly where Rip lived on Mask Road. She had done some Internet research and driven by in her sperm decision-making days. Rip had a very nice little house in a trendy new development. It was a beige brick and stucco one story with black window frames—very manly. She was curious to see inside.

She parked her car in his driveway and followed the curved walkway to the front door. Before she had a chance to ring the doorbell, Rip opened the door and greeted her with a smile.

Yes, the sweater was a good idea.

Rip was dressed in gray shorts and a navy T-shirt. And muscle. Lots of lovely muscle. She stepped in, brushed his chest (accidentally on purpose), and breathed in his matching musky pheromones. Together they would make a wonderful moldy side dish. She looked at his wavy black hair and the interest in his dark eyes. Side dish? No, definitely a main dish.

A little tinker bell rang in her head. One, she was ten days away from having Jared's baby. And two, much as their musky scents were compatible, look what happened with Roger. For four years she had wined and dined the dream of settling down with him, and in the end it was a bust. She didn't want to go through that again. She liked the surefire plan of having a baby with Jared. He hadn't come back for his sperm, thankfully, so it was a go. She eyed Rip with a twinge of regret. Their gametes would never meet, it was a little sad. But she'd stick with her plan.

"Come on in, Chloe."

He led her past the living room. Chloe had a quick impression of two leather recliners, bookshelves, and a large television. They continued down the hall to the kitchen. Light streamed in a large picture window overlooking the backyard. A warm breeze lifted the curtains on a side window in the eating area, and low blues music filled the air.

"I thought we could sit outside," Rip said. "Can I get you a drink? Beer? Wine?"

Chloe eyed the open beer on the counter. "Do you have a soft drink? I drove over." She set her purse down on the chunky wooden table in the eating area.

Rip poked his head in the fridge. "Root beer?"

"Love it." She looked around and sniffed the air. "Something smells delicious."

Rip poured the root beer in a glass with ice and handed it to her. "Homemade lasagna."

Chloe's eyebrows shot up. "Impressive."

"Not my home," he said with a grin. "Franco's makes the best homemade lasagna. I figure we should all stick to what we're good at." Rip gestured to a French door off the eating area. "This way . . ."

Chloe stepped out onto a wooden deck, surprised that the quiet sound of blues music carried outside. Rip guided her past a small stone table set for two to a set of patio chairs. Chloe sank into the plush cushion and looked around.

A grand maple tree in the middle of the backyard filtered sunshine to the rest of the lawn. A wooden fence on the perimeter was partially hidden by a garden filled with shrubs, low ground cover, and a few scattered geraniums, and a hot tub looked inviting, tucked into the edge of the deck on the right.

"It's a little oasis," Chloe said.

Rip nodded. "I was lucky to get this place. I don't have any neighbors to the right, and beyond the property line at the back, there's a small stream."

"A waterfront property," Chloe said with a grin. "Looks like you have quite the green thumb, too."

"Nope. My mom comes over a couple of times in the summer to garden. Her own isn't big enough."

"Perfect set up."

Rip took a sip of beer. "Tell me what has you worried."

Chloe looked over at him. "You know how they say eavesdroppers never hear anything good?" She sat a bit straighter. "I think they're wrong."

Rip tilted his head and smiled. "I think that's 'eavesdroppers never hear anything good about themselves.'"

"Oh. Well. Good thing it wasn't about me then." Chloe swirled the ice in her drink. "I told you that last week I painted a storage room at Weed 'n Feed."

Rip nodded.

"Well, when I was there, I . . ." Chloe looked around. "Nobody can hear us, right?"

"No, it's okay. We're far enough away."

"K good. When I was there I overheard this really creepy voice threatening Chris Bellantine, the owner."

Rip watched her closely. "What did you hear? Can you repeat it exactly?"

"It was like 'I can take fifty grams of weed or fifty grams of your face. You choose.'" Chloe mimicked the gravelly voice.

"It was a male voice?"

"Yes."

"Did the two men know each other?"

"I think so. Chris Bellantine didn't seem too happy, but he didn't question who the guy was. At least, not from what I heard."

"Did you see him? Did he see you?"

"No and no. They were talking in the hallway. I was in the storage room."

"Okay. Go on."

"Today I went out to lunch with Ruby, you know, the woman who's going to live in the barn." At Rip's nod, she continued. "A couple she knows named Millie and Merv Preston started a little restaurant business at their farm. Presto, it's called. We went there for lunch and when we were there"—her eyes widened—"I heard the voice again."

"The same voice? Are you sure?"

Chloe nodded. "I didn't see him, but it was his voice. Definitely. And he didn't sound too happy this time either. He could really benefit from a life coach." She took a sip of her root beer. "He was threatening Merv."

"The guy who owns the place? How so?"

"Yes. It sounded like he lent Merv money in exchange for lacing the food with marijuana, and when Merv said he didn't want to do it anymore, the guy demanded a huge amount of money."

Rip looked thoughtful. "You're sure about this?"

"Yes. The menu had little green leafy symbols beside some of the items. I didn't realize what it meant at the time. But the brownies were six dollars. Isn't that outrageous? Six dollars."

"Pot-laced brownies. A little something extra. Do you think Millie is baking with weed or are they just a handy outlet?"

Chloe bit her lip. "I don't know. Ruby was worried about Millie—said she was more stressed lately. Ruby figured it was due to the restaurant, but I don't think she suspected this. And when I heard that voice, I didn't want to ask her or involve her. The guy was scary creepy."

"Smart. I'm glad you called me. Do you think you could recognize the voice again?"

"Without a doubt."

"Let me make a call and set it up. We'll have to go to the station to keep it official, but we could eat dinner first."

Chloe beamed. "The police version of 'He said. She said.'" She brought her glass to her lips and looked at him. "What's the prize if I get it right?"

Rip's eyes roamed down to her chest and back. "A hot night in a Bennett suite?"

Chloe gulped her root beer. She'd better stick with free pizza.

# Chapter 16

Chloe sat across from Rip at the little table outside, a candle flickering between them, eating the lasagna and garlic toast. Normally she wouldn't go anywhere near garlic on a date, just in case. But the more time she spent with Rip, the more she wished his sperm were still available. She was told no sex the week before insemination, so she had a few extra helpings of garlic toast to keep him at a distance.

Chloe wiped her mouth on a napkin and sat back. "That was delicious. Thank you very much."

"My pleasure. Why don't we head to the station and then come back for dessert later?"

"You have dessert?"

Rip laughed. "Or you can have dessert now."

"No, after sounds good. I'm stuffed."

Rip blew out the candle, and they collected the plates and carried them inside.

"The station's only a ten-minute walk away, if you feel up to it. Or I can call a cab. I've only had one beer, but I don't want to drink and drive."

"A walk sounds lovely."

Chloe grabbed her purse, and Rip locked the door behind them. He pointed the way and slipped his hand in hers as they walked. Rip waved hello to a couple of neighbors as they passed.

"This is a pretty neighborhood. Is it new?" Chloe asked.

"Fairly. It was built about five years ago. I moved in last year."

They arrived at the station, and Rip held the door open for Chloe and led the way down a hallway to an unmarked door. He swiped a pass and the door unlocked.

The room beyond was an open space with cubicles around the perimeter. Rip greeted two officers working at the desks. They looked at Chloe with curious eyes, and smiled her way, but Rip guided Chloe toward an office at one end of the room.

"This is my office, but we'll head to the room next door." He pointed to a door off to the right and with another swipe of his pass, they walked in.

An officer in uniform stood up as they entered.

Rip held out his hand. "Trevor, thanks for setting this up."

"Happy to do it." Trevor shook Rip's hand and glanced at Chloe.

"Chloe, this is Detective Trevor Hughes. Chloe Keay."

Blue eyes focused on her. They were friendly, but she stepped a little closer to Rip for comfort. She held out her hand. "Pleased to meet you."

"Same. Have a seat." He gestured to a chair opposite his across a metal table. "Rip's filled in the background, and we can type up your statement and get you to sign it a little later. For now, we'd like to nail down the voice. I'll play six voices, and we'll see if any of them match what you heard." He adjusted a control. "Do you have any questions?"

"No, I don't think so." She glanced over at Rip, who stood against the wall and reassured her with a smile.

Trevor played the first voice. Chloe frowned and shook her head. "That's not it."

Trevor nodded once and played the second voice. Chloe's eyebrows went up. "That's the fellow Rip just said hi to out there. Not the same voice I overheard."

Trevor gave a slight smile and nodded. "Okay. How about this one?"

Chloe listened, but the voice wasn't quite the same. "No."

"Number four."

Chloe listened to the gravelly voice and knew that was it. She looked over at Rip. "That's the one. That's him."

"Are you sure?" Trevor asked.

"Yes, I'd recognize it anywhere. That's the guy I overheard at Weed 'n Feed and talking to Merv at Presto."

A silent look passed between Rip and Trevor. Chloe watched Trevor give an imperceptible nod, and Rip answered with a grim tightening of his lips. Then Rip's features relaxed and he pushed off against the wall to straighten. "Thanks Chloe, that's very helpful."

"Is he as creepy as he sounds?"

"Yes, he's not the kind of guy you'd want to hang around."

"Are you after him?"

"Yes, and this really helps us. Would you give your statement to Trevor? Tell him exactly what happened?"

"Yes, of course. Anything to help."

They spent another hour. Trevor took down the information, and Chloe read it over and signed. When she was done, Trevor led her back to Rip's office.

Staff Sergeant Ripley Logan, Chloe read on the door. Rip looked so official and very sexy sitting behind his desk flipping through a sheaf of papers. He put them down and stood up as she entered.

Trevor gave a small salute. "Thanks again, Chloe." He turned to Rip. "We'll talk."

Rip nodded to him and came to stand beside Chloe. "How'd it go?"

"Good. I think he recorded every sigh and blink. He's very thorough." A little bit of OCD there, she thought, but didn't want to insult Rip's friend.

Rip looked at her sympathetically. "He is. I'm sorry to put you through that, but it really does help."

Chloe waved it away. "No worries. I'm happy to do it. But I have to warn you I'm better with voices than words."

"That's okay. It's all part of a bigger picture. Ready to go? We can head back to my place. How does peach pie sound?"

"Oh." She wiggled her eyebrows. "Heavenly. With vanilla ice cream?"

"With vanilla ice cream," he said with a smile.

The sun was setting and the streetlights lit the sidewalk on their way home as they walked hand in hand.

Chloe shivered.

"Cold?" Rip asked.

"A little."

He put an arm around her shoulders and held her close. "The evenings are getting cooler."

Chloe pulled the edges of her sweater together and snuggled closer. She rubbed against his chest and enjoyed the feel of the taut muscles of his thigh. He'd probably look delicious naked.

Rip unlocked the door to his house and ushered her inside. She shivered again when he moved away.

"Jeez, you're really cold." He ran his hand lightly down her arm.

Chloe suppressed another shiver. That one wasn't from cold.

"Would you like to sit in the hot tub for a bit? Get warmed up?"

Chloe considered. Would Rip join her? Relaxing in bubbly hot water across from that. She mentally raked her eyes up and down Rip's muscular body. Big yes. However, no sex the week before Jared's sperm. Hmmm. She'd have to be strong. She could look, no touching. Her breath caught in her chest. Even a look would be great. And wouldn't that be just the thing her ovaries needed? She could practically feel them releasing eggs as she pondered.

Rip stepped closer. "I have a swimsuit you could borrow." He leaned in and brushed his lips softly against hers.

She shivered again.

Rip took her hand and walked down the hall to his bedroom. He reached in his closet and pulled out a canvas bag. "There should be something in here you could wear. I started a collection of stuff people left behind." He pulled a silk dressing gown off a hook and handed it to her. "You can wear this. I'll get the pie."

He strode out of the room, and Chloe brought the fabric to her nose and sniffed the musky scent. She couldn't wait to wrap herself in that. She sorted through the swimsuits in the bag. His previous guests had much smaller chests. She finally selected a bikini that covered her bottom, and a top with two little triangles of fabric that left a lot of exposed skin. She hoped for low lighting.

She wrapped herself in the dressing gown and belted it around her waist and headed to the kitchen.

Rip stood at the counter in black swimming trunks. Her mouth went dry. That was under the T-shirt? Why would he ever cover that up? His skin was tanned, his chest smooth, and the muscles of his abdomen rippled when he moved. Her nipples tightened through the silk as she watched him.

She walked in, and he looked up. "Find something that fit?"

"As long as I don't move around too much, I should be fine."

"No swimming lengths in the hot tub." He set two plates on a tray. "I made some hot chocolate."

He added two mugs and a candle to the tray and carried it out the French door to the deck. He set the tray down on a ledge beside the hot tub and lifted the cover off the tub. A pouf of steam rose in the air, and he adjusted the controls so colored light filled the tub. Chloe unbelted the robe and shrugged it off her shoulders. She sat down on the ledge beside the tray and dipped her feet in the swirling water.

Rip stopped her with a touch on her arm. "You look beautiful. I think that fits perfectly." Chloe's heart skipped at the look in his eyes. He stroked his hand down her arm and held her elbow firmly as she sank into the water. Rip walked over and pressed a remote so quiet music filled the air. Then he stepped in and sat down beside her.

"Feels good at the end of the day," he said looking over at her. "Let me know if you still need help warming up."

Chloe shook her head. She'd stopped needing help with that the moment she'd seen his naked chest in the kitchen.

"Would you like the pie before the ice cream melts?" He handed her a plate and took his own. They sat eating as music played in the background.

"Delicious," she said as she scooped the last crumb from her plate. She turned and set the empty plate on the ledge.

Rip added his to the tray and then turned to face her. "Hold on. You have a crumb here." He leaned over and brushed his lips against hers. He sat back at eye level and looked at her. "Sorry, I forgot the napkins."

She sat still, her lips tingling when he pulled away. ". . . save a tree."

Rip grinned and handed her a mug. He looked at her over the rim as he took a sip. "I'm glad you contacted me." He paused. "Your instincts were correct, and if you hear the voice again, don't go near him. He's been on our radar lately. If you think there's a chance he saw you, we should provide some protection for you."

Chloe watched the bubbles rise in the water. "No, I'm sure he didn't. I don't think that's necessary. I'll keep your phone number handy though, just in case."

"Absolutely. Call any time. Day or night."

Chloe looked at the slick skin of his bare chest. He probably didn't mean it that way. "So, what's your position on babies?"

Rip's eyebrows went up. "Babies? Can't say I've had much experience with them. Although I do like the process of creating them."

Chloe laughed. "I just wondered if you see children in your future."

Rip sobered. "No." He swirled the drink in his hands. "I don't."

Chloe blinked. No dilly-dallying there. "Really? Never?"

He gave a quick shake of his head. "No."

Don't want to talk about it, Chloe read loud and clear. Why? Why not? You have some of the best genes in the gene pool, she thought with frustration. What was with these guys? Don't they want a little bambino to cuddle? Was she the only one who felt that clock ticking?

She straightened her shoulders. Well, good to know now. Luckily, she had a backup plan that was progressing nicely. She just had to stay on track.

She looked at his dark eyes and square jaw, even sexier when he brooded. Broad shoulders, the bulging muscles of his arms, the very sexy sculpted abdomen slipping under the water. A twinge of sadness squeezed her heart. A gorgeous bod and a sexy personality to boot. Kind, gentle, considerate, fun. She could wake up to that every day.

Wow. That was a first. No doubt, no question, it could be forever.

Even with Roger, sadly, she had wondered about forever. Maybe that's why she hadn't pushed too hard for more.

But no bambinos? She sighed. That was a deal breaker. She couldn't picture a future without the patter of little feet. She glanced at Rip with an ache in her chest. It wasn't meant to be. She'd carry on solo.

She cleared her throat. "Well, I guess it's not for everyone. How's your baseball team doing?"

Rip looked over quietly for a moment and then seemed to shake himself. "Good, good. Haven't busted any windshields lately."

"What? No home runs?"

"I put police tape across the entrance to the north parking lot." He smiled and brushed the hair away from her face. "Although, that's how I met the most beautiful person I know."

Chloe melted. Was a retirement plan really all that important?

# Chapter 17

The next day at work, Chloe's skin still tingled whenever she thought about Rip. She had finished her hot chocolate and reluctantly dressed. With a quick peck on his cheek, she had said good-bye and headed home to her bed, alone.

A plan was in place, and she was going to see it through. She had done all that soul searching with Roger. Been there, done that. She wanted kids. Even if all they did was poop and sleep, she was ready to be a mother. She was ready to kiss their booboos better and snuggle, cuddle, and nurture them to the greatness they were destined to achieve. She watched April and Scott raise Ava, was a part of Taryn's life, and knew it wasn't all peaches and cream, but she was ready and willing to make the sacrifices to put a baby first.

And hopefully, some time in her future, a man would come along and want that too.

Plus, you know, financial security. It really was the perfect plan.

Except it wasn't going to include Rip.

She stirred the paint and poured it into a tray.

Her family, well Pamela, had organized a little shindig for her thirtieth birthday. Thirty already. Jeez. Hope those eggs were still popping. Although if the image of a naked-from-the-waist-up Rip didn't get them stirred up, nothing would.

Yes, so the party. A little get-together, on Wednesday night, at her parent's retirement home to celebrate her and Cory's birthday. Pizza, cake, possibly streamers and balloons.

Chloe rolled builder's beige on the wall, moving in a V from floor to ceiling.

She couldn't quite come to grips with never seeing Rip again, so that morning, after ruminating half the night about it, she'd texted him and asked if he'd like to go. And he said yes.

He'd said yes, she still couldn't quite believe it. It had taken ages to convince Roger to meet her family. 'Course Roger was a dope.

It really was such a shame about Rip's no-baby policy. Chloe sighed. Ah well, we all had our flaws.

She dipped the roller in the tray and rolled off the excess paint. Good thing she liked boring builder's beige. Today was the first day of an eight-week stretch painting for Bennett Homes. Another subdivision. Rivermede was still growing—it was good for the economy and even better for her bank account.

Bennett Homes always left the painting for last. All the other trades were done and gone. It saved the hassle of touch-ups if the walls were accidentally dinged, but it made for a long quiet day. She adjusted the ear buds, listening to music.

The first few notes of 'Love Shack' played on the radio. Chloe squealed and set down her roller. How could you not dance to this? She turned the volume up and threw her arms in the air. Hips gyrating and feet moving, she moved with the music. She did her signature move, miming opening the refrigerator door and then closing it. Opening the freezer door, then closing it. Head bobbing and arms flailing, she kept it up until the song ended. "Oh, that's so fun. What a great song!"

She picked up her roller again. It was like having a seventh inning stretch to keep her going.

She finished the first bedroom and was setting up in the second when she heard a knock on the door.

"Hello-o! Chloe?"

Margo. "I'm up here." She pulled out her ear buds and walked into the hallway.

Margo skipped up the stairs. "Hi, Chloe." She moved closer for a hug.

Chloe grinned as she squeezed back. "Playing hooky already?"

"I have this afternoon off. It's a trade-off for working evenings at the Sexual Health Clinic. Officially sanctioned study time."

"Nice. We do like our doctors to be studied."

Margo laughed and shook her head. "How's the painting going?"

"Great. I just started here today. Reams and reams of builder's beige, but at least it makes for easy clean up. How's the residency going? You look glowy."

"Glowy? Yeah, I guess I feel glowy."

"That probably has more to do with the Bennett heir, I imagine," said Chloe, with a wink.

"Yes, you'd be right about that. But the medicine is good. I'm glad I went back."

Chloe nodded. Of course. Everyone except Margo had seen it. It had taken a year away from medicine, some painting, and some soul searching for her to get to that point. "I'm glad it's working out. And speaking of the Bennett heir, how is Trace?"

"He's great. He started classes after a week of orientation and fun stuff."

"Jumped right in."

"Yup, that hasn't changed. Classes from eight thirty 'til four thirty. But he's still on cloud nine, loving it," Margo said.

"You sound surprised."

Margo winced. "Sorry, I have to watch that. Not everyone will have the same experience as me, I know. And Trace won't. He absolutely loves it."

"And you."

Margo looked smug. "And me." She smiled. "And how are things with you? Have you, you know—"

"Snagged the sperm?" Chloe asked with a grin. "Not yet, but it's all picked out and the big day is next Wednesday."

"Next week? Wow. You're really going to do this?"

"Really am. I am so ready. Hey, we're having a family party tomorrow night to celebrate my birthday— the big three-O. You want to come?"

"I'd love to, but they stick the first-year family medicine residents at the Sexual Health Clinic on Wednesday nights. I'm sorry. But I could buy you lunch next Thursday to celebrate instead."

"Excellent. I'd love that."

Margo nodded. "It's a date. I've got to run. I just dropped by to see how you're doing, but it looks like everything's under control. If you need a hand or get swamped, let me know. There's a bit of flexibility in my schedule, especially on the weekends."

"Thanks, Margo. I appreciate it. Right now it's good, but I'll keep it in mind."

Margo leaned over to hug her again. "Next Thursday, then."

"Me and the bambino will be there."

Margo looked startled for a moment and then laughed. "Love you, Mommy."

"Love you, too."

With a grin and wave, Margo headed back down the stairs and out the door.

Chloe picked up the roller. Mommy. It had a nice ring to it.

# Chapter 18

Chloe pulled into the convenience store parking lot. There was just enough time to buy a lottery ticket before she picked up Rip and drove out to the retirement home.

"Hello there, birthday girl," said Bea. "Don't you look lovely tonight. Thirty obviously suits you."

Chloe smiled. "Why thank you, Bea." She twirled around and made the hem of the bright purple skirt flare around her thighs. "It's a circle skirt."

"It flies up just enough to be interesting. Who're you dressing up for tonight, sugar pie?"

"His name's Rip. A birthday present for myself."

"You hired a hooker?" Bea asked, her eyes wide.

"I think that would be a male escort. But no. He's a friend. A very hunky, gorgeous friend."

Bea wiggled her eyebrows. "A friend with benefits?"

Chloe shook her head. "Bea. Really."

"What? Looking at a hunky handsome all evening would be a benefit."

"Oh, then yes. There is a definite benefit. I'll need an extra one tonight," she said as Bea printed off the lottery ticket. "It's Cory's birthday, too."

Bea handed her two lottery tickets. "Here's one for Cory, and this one for you is on me. Don't mix 'em up. You don't want Cory winning your millions. Happy Birthday."

"Aw. Thank you. You're a sweetie." Chloe skipped around the counter, gave Bea a quick hug, and handed her the money for Cory's ticket. "Wish us luck."

Bea eyed Chloe from head to toe. "Somebody's gonna get lucky."

Chloe chuckled and backed away. "I like to drive the men wild."

"Everybody loves you, honey. You have a fun birthday."

"Thanks, Bea." With a wave, Chloe skipped out again and settled in her car.

She pulled into Rip's driveway and before she had the car in park, Rip came out the front door. Chloe tingled again.

He wore long pants that hugged his thighs and showed off bulging muscle. A dark T-shirt stretched across broad shoulders. Chloe wished she could run her hands down his chest to see if it felt as hard as it looked.

Rip smiled as he walked over and pulled open the passenger door. "Hi, Chloe. You don't mind driving?"

"Not at all. My dad'll be happy to see the car. It's his baby. You look great."

"Thanks. You look beautiful. Happy Birthday." He leaned over and kissed her cheek.

Chloe caught the scent of fresh soap and sighed with pleasure. "Thank you."

Rip sat back and fastened his seat belt. "Catch me up on your family. Who will be there tonight?"

Chloe put the car in gear and backed out. "The whole clan, I think. I have five sibs. Dale, married to Natalie. They have two sons, Ben and Joey. Then there's Pamela—she's pregnant, about four months along, and her husband Rod, Devon and his partner Adrian, April, her husband Scott, and their four-year-old daughter Ava, and Cory, my twin."

"You have a twin?"

"Fraternal, obviously. He's a boy. His girlfriend should be there, too. Her name's Janet."

"Big group."

"Yeah. Don't worry if you can't keep them all straight. My parents have trained us to respond to any term of endearment."

"I'll keep that in mind, love."

Chloe felt a swirl in her heart. Coming from him was totally different from the 'I can't quite remember your name' Mom and Dad version.

Chloe cleared her throat and glanced over at him. "Thanks for coming with me tonight."

"My pleasure."

She pulled in to her parents' retirement place and parked between a Celica and a Mustang. "Looks like Cory and Devon are here," she said.

"Old sports cars run in your family?" Rip asked.

"My dad's hobby. We're not really into exchanging gifts for holidays, except for our twenty-first birthday. My dad picks out and fixes up a vintage car for us. It's the best birthday gift ever."

"A stylish set of wheels. Nice."

"Yeah. And the biggest bonus? I can pick my car out of a packed parking lot."

They walked toward the front entrance of the building, and Chloe smiled at the couple sitting outside enjoying the evening. The sun was getting low, but the warmth from the day still reflected off the pavement.

They made their way to the private dining room, and Chloe smiled at the decorations hanging on the walls. They were the same ones used at the thirtieth birthday parties for Dale, Pamela, Devon, and April. Frugal and festive—the best kind of party.

Chloe linked her hand with Rip's and drew him inside. The smell of spicy pizza filled the air, and a birthday cake, with a lot of candles on top, graced the side table. The usual array of raw vegetables, standing on end in small glass vases, along with dip in individual shot glasses, looked tasty and very healthy beside the pizza. That would be Pamela's touch. She tended to guilt everyone into eating two carrot sticks before they were allowed their share of dessert.

A chorus of happy birthdays greeted Chloe when she walked into the room. Chloe smiled back and introduced Rip to the group.

Rip nodded to the kids, shook hands with the adults, and gently kissed Joy's cheek. "I see now where Chloe gets her youthful beauty," he said as he drew back.

Chloe watched her mom's eyes go from curious hesitation to watchful consideration to warm approval. A little compliment went a long way.

Chloe gave Cory a close hug. "Happy Birthday, big brother."

Cory laughed. "One more year older and wiser."

They sat down, some with napkins on their laps, some around the table in the middle of the room, and devoured five large pizzas and all of the carrot sticks. After Chloe made a wish (a healthy tiny tot with a small head to make the whole fitting-through-the-birth-canal thing a little easier), she and Cory blew out the candles on the cake (over the years Pamela had calmed down with the 'you're blowing germs all over everyone's food' speech).

Then it was time to open the cards. Ava jumped up and down, and with an excited grin, she handed hers to Chloe. Chloe opened it and took out the lottery ticket.

"We got you ice cream. Lots and lots of ice cream for a whole year," Ava said.

"Enough that I can share it with you?" Chloe asked as she gathered her close for a hug.

"Yes, enough for everyone."

"Hey, I think that's what you gave Grandma and me, too," Chloe's dad said.

"Yes and Cory, too."

Everyone joined in the laughter.

Pamela handed Chloe a card. When Chloe lifted out the lottery ticket and looked over, Pamela said, "I'm adding a guest room for you on our house. I'd like you to be godparent and spend a lot of time with us."

Chloe felt her eyes fill. Before the tears could spill over, she jumped up and went over to hug Pamela. "Thank you. I'd be honored to be godparent."

Pamela gave her a watery smile. "I figure it would be a good balance to my serious parenting."

"I'd be delighted to share my sweet tooth and candy-floss cravings with your baby."

Pamela looked stricken for a moment and then rolled her eyes. "I was thinking more like rollerblading and playing tag."

"Oh, I can do that, too."

Pamela laughed and rubbed her belly.

Next, Ben and Joey handed Chloe an envelope. She lifted out the lottery ticket and looked at them with her eyebrows raised.

"It's a vacation," Ben said.

"Dad says someplace warm. Mom said snowboarding with Alf," added Joey.

Ben looked at him. "Alps," he corrected.

Joey looked at Chloe with a grin. "Alps."

Chloe hugged them both. "Maybe I'll win enough to afford both."

Devon bought her a shopping spree at her favorite clothing store, and Cory looked at her with amusement dancing in his eyes as he handed her a card. "I got you a karaoke machine with a huge selection of song lyrics." He laughed. "So maybe you'll get them right."

Chloe wrinkled her nose at him and kissed his cheek. "Thank you. Even if my version is usually better."

They went around again giving cards with wishes to Cory.

Chloe snagged another piece of cake and sat back and enjoyed the chatter while she ate. Rip sat beside her and occasionally stroked her hair or touched her arm, sending tingles down her spine. She leaned into him once and looked over to laugh with him when the boys gave Cory the wish of a pinball machine. Her breath caught at the look in his eyes, and a zing of electricity shot threw her. He wanted her. She glanced around the room wondering if anyone else felt the heat, but they were watching Cory. Good thing. She felt a few of her brain cells sizzle.

She inched away and told herself to focus on Jared's sperm.

They finished eating, and when her mom and dad started to fade, they collected the plates and began to tidy the room. Chloe and Cory got a bye from cleanup duties, so they escorted their parents back to their suite.

"Rip seems like a very nice boy. I like him," Joy said as they walked arm-in-arm along the long hallway.

"I really like him, too," Chloe said.

"But. I sense a but."

"But he doesn't want kids, Mom."

Joy squeezed Chloe's arm. "How do you find all these men who don't want babies?"

Chloe gave a short laugh. "I don't know." She leaned her head against her mom briefly. "How can they know? Did Dad want kids? Did you plan a big family?"

"I think he did. Did we talk about it—let me think. Maybe I just assumed he did," she said with a laugh. "No, I'm sure. I didn't get pregnant with Dale right away. Pamela was a bit of a miscalculation. Devon and April we planned, and then after you two, I'd had enough and we were a lot more careful with birth control. It wasn't as easy thirty years ago. The pill was a little riskier. But pregnancy was even more so, and six babies was enough for me."

"I don't want to fall in love with someone who doesn't want children."

Her mom glanced at her but didn't say anything.

Chloe closed her eyes briefly at the sympathy she saw. "I know. It may be too late." She squeezed her mom close. "It'll all work out the way it's supposed to, right Ma?"

"It will," her mom said. "Happy Birthday, sweetheart."

"Thanks, Mom." She kissed her cheek. "I love you."

"Love you, too."

Chloe kissed her dad and walked back to the party room with Cory. "You off with Janet?"

Cory wiggled his eyebrows. "Hoping for one more birthday gift."

Chloe laughed and punched his arm. "You have a one-track mind."

"Of course. I'm male."

When they returned to the party room, the decorations were down and the food cleared away. Rip and Janet were the only ones left.

Rip handed the leftover cake to Chloe. "They cleaned up and headed out, but the kids were certain you'd want this."

"The kids were right," she said and planted a quick kiss on his cheek. "Thanks for coming tonight."

"I enjoyed it. Your family is great."

Chloe nodded. "I'm lucky."

She waved good-bye to Cory and Janet and linked her arm with Rip's.

"I have one more gift for you at home," Rip said as they walked out.

Chloe's heart stumbled. Did he compare notes with Janet? "You didn't have to do that."

He shrugged. "I wanted to. And this gift is as much for me as it is for you."

Chloe swallowed. She pictured him naked in the hot tub and her pulse started racing. Hot diggity dog. How could she work in that she was saving herself for Jared's sperm?

# Chapter 19

Rip unlocked his front door and gestured for her to go inside. She turned slightly and brushed her breasts against his chest.

If a spike of hormones popped the DNA jelly-bellies from her ovaries, she was going to have a windfall of them tumbling down her tubes waiting for Jared's sperm. She'd better take it down a notch or she'd be having triplets.

"Would you like something to drink?" Rip asked, heading to the kitchen.

Yes. Yes, she would. But she still had to drive home. What would be a good sex deterrent? "Tea would be nice."

Rip nodded and pulled a kettle out of a cabinet, filled it with water, and plugged it in. He opened another cabinet and pulled out three boxes of tea bags. "Sleepytime, Orange Pekoe, or Rise and Shine. I think that one is citrus," he said, reading the label on the box.

Rise and shine? Really? There was a tea for sex? The room suddenly felt very warm. What was next—wet and wild blueberry? "Orange Pekoe is good," she managed, squirming.

Rip turned to her. "Would you like your gift while we're waiting for the kettle to boil?"

Chloe swallowed. Maybe.

Rip smiled and planted a light kiss on her lips. "I'll be right back."

Chloe plunked down on one of the bar stools. Sexy with a capital S. Man, he was hot. Whew.

Rip returned to the kitchen carrying an envelope. "For you."

Chloe eyed it suspiciously and then took it from his hand. She shook it, and Rip laughed.

"It's an envelope. Why are you shaking it?"

"You never know. Don't like to judge a book by its cover."

Chloe opened the card and read what he had written.

"Ah thank you." She pulled a smaller envelope from inside the card. "This isn't one of those Russian doll-type cards, is it? Small and smaller cards until poof, nothing."

He laughed. "No, there is something in that one."

Chloe pulled out two tickets to see Jeremy Jamieson, a hot new country and western singer. "Holy moly. How did you get these? They were sold out before I could log on last week."

He shrugged and smiled. "You just need to know the right people."

She did a little jig, threw her arms in the air, and then jumped into Rip's arms and gave him a tight hug. "Thank you so much. I was dying to go to his concert." She pulled back. "His 'Leave It to Believe It' song is one of my favorites."

Rip laughed. "I love you," he said, shaking his head.

Chloe stilled. She looked him in the eye. "Wh—what did you say?"

Rip's smile froze and a flush crept up his neck. "Ah, I said you're going to love it. He puts on a great show."

Chloe looked at the tickets and nodded slowly. "Yeah. Have you seen him before?"

Rip grimaced. "Well, no actually. But I've heard."

The kettle whistled loudly and with a look of relief, Rip turned to pour the water into a mug and added a tea bag. He handed it to Chloe and then made himself a coffee. "Would you like to sit outside?"

They settled into the deck chairs. Crickets chirped and leaves rustled quietly in the night. Small lights around the garden lit the backyard and created leafy patterns on the fence.

Rip sipped his coffee. "So, what did you wish for when you blew out the candles?"

"Can't tell. Then it wouldn't come true."

"You believe that?"

"For sure." She nodded. "Number one rule for wishes and luck."

"What's rule number two?"

"Buy a ticket. Can't win it if you're not in it."

"Very wise." He nodded sagely. "Your family must have shares in the lottery business."

She grinned at him. "We would if we could."

"Has anyone ever won anything?"

"Devon won fifty thousand once."

"Wow."

"I know. And we win enough free plays and five dollar prizes to keep us playing."

"What would you buy if you won?"

"Me?" She sipped her tea. "If I won really big? First, I'd put some away for retirement." She glanced at him. "Apparently, that's a big concern. And after driving Smitty's convertible, which I loved, I'd probably splurge a little and get a second car. Don't want to hurt Dad's feelings, but sailing along with the top down was pretty nice. And then, you know, share it with family, take a long vacation. What would you do if you won?"

"Man, I hardly ever buy a lottery ticket." He leaned back in the lounger. "If it was a million or more, I'd probably retire. Invest some, spend some. I'd like to see Hawaii and learn how to surf. And I'd donate to the Cancer Society."

"I'll go to Hawaii with you."

"Deal." He paused. "Chloe, there's something I want to tell you."

Chloe stilled at the serious tone. It didn't sound as if she was going to like it. Her heart rate kicked up.

"You know how I told you that Smitty would lend you a car while your windshield was getting fixed?" he asked.

"Yeah."

"Well actually, Smitty doesn't have a loaner car. His business doesn't usually need one. The Miata is mine."

Chloe jerked back. "Yours? Why would you lend me your car?"

"So we could put a GPS tracker on it and monitor your movements." He put his coffee cup on the floor beside his chair.

"Me?" she said, her voice rising. "Why?"

"We wondered if you were part of a drug cartel plot."

"Really?" Chloe grinned from ear to ear. "Drug cartel?" She laughed. "That's great. Did I live up to your expectations?"

"Well, let's just say you're not what I expected." He looked down at his hands. "But after you tipped us off about Giuseppe—"

"Giuseppe?"

"The man behind the voice you heard at Weed 'n Feed and Presto."

"Ohhh. Creepy Guy."

Rip smiled. "Yeah, Creepy Guy. He's a suspect in a major drug operation."

"Is Merv going to be safe?"

He nodded. "It'll shake itself out in a day or two. I don't want to scare you, but for the next twenty-four to forty-eight hours, be aware of your surroundings. If you feel uneasy at all, give me a call."

Chloe shuddered. "Sounds ominous."

"It'll be fine. It's just a precaution."

"Okay." She wrapped her hands around her mug. "So, a tracker, eh?"

He nodded. "You buy a lot of lottery tickets. And you really should use Google maps. You take the most inefficient routes to places."

"It's not about the destination, it's about the journey."

"But think of all the extra time you would have if you were more efficient."

"What would I do with extra time?"

He looked at her with a twinkle in his eye. "I can think of a few things."

Chloe looked at him and grinned. Another birthday wish might come true.

# Chapter 20

Rip watched Chloe get in her car and wave good-bye. He needed a cold shower. They'd only shared a kiss, but the thought of going further, filling his hands with those breasts, exploring those curves. Yeah, he needed a cold shower.

He couldn't believe he blurted out that he loved her. Man. It slipped out. He rubbed his chest at the ache that started. He did love her, God help him. She was sweet, a little quirky mind you, but kind and generous. With a killer body and a promise of fun. He couldn't ever see life getting boring or stale with her around. She breezed in, swirled her citrus perfume around his heart, and took it with her. She was it.

Hell, he even liked her family.

He was in it for the whole nine yards, but her deer-caught-in-headlights response had him backpedaling. Her heart wasn't quite his yet. And she seemed pretty bent on having kids. His heart ached again. He hoped that wasn't a deal breaker.

Maybe she needed romance. Flowers. Chocolate. The promise to drive his Miata. That might work.

He stepped back inside and shut the door as his phone vibrated with a text. Work. As effective as a cold shower.

It looked like it was a go for tonight.

The surveillance on Giuseppe paid off, and the warrant for his arrest came through. Tonight was the night.

Rip fired off a text to the rest of the TRU team to meet at the office at 2 a.m. in field greens, and dialed the number of the investigating officer in the drug unit to set the wheels in motion.


Rip sipped his coffee and listened as Mac and Dub ironed out the last of the details. Mac, or Paul MacKinnet, was the Sierra Element leader. His team would be on the ground while Steve Westminster, Dub for short, and the rest of the Alpha Team breached the premises and made the arrest. The canine unit was built into the plan because Juan Giuseppe, target suspect, managed to buy himself a big ass house with four entry points.

Rip, Mac, Dub, and Shirk, TRU team Sergeant Dirk Shannon, had spent the last sixty minutes in Rip's office going over the content of the surveillance tapes and looking at the floor plans for the house.

Out of the corner of his eye, Rip saw Frenzy walk in, coffee in hand. That was everyone. He glanced at the time. 1:55 a.m.

He stood up. "Let's go brief the team."

His office was adjacent to Shirk's and outside their doors, the room opened up to a larger space with enough desks and cubicles around the periphery for the ten first-class constables who made up the team. The men stood around chatting with each other. Frenzy sat back with his feet up on a desk, waiting.

Mac and Dub walked out and joined the rest of the team. Conversations trailed off, and the constables pulled their chairs around to face Rip's office and sat down. Shirk leaned against the wall on one side of a large white board, which hung between their offices and doubled as a screen. Rip stood on the other side and started the briefing.

"Juan Giuseppe is the target." Giuseppe's face filled the screen, left profile, right profile, full facial shot, and three more slides taken from the surveillance video. "This isn't the first time through this for most of you, but I'll go over it again. Giuseppe's the local right-hand man of the Stirling drug cartel. He's not the top henchman but close enough that we're hoping his arrest will cascade into others. He's considered armed and dangerous. His aliases are listed here." He flashed another screen. "Seems like anything starting with the letter G." Rip took a sip of coffee. "He has a long list of priors, mainly possession and trafficking. This time his name is linked with the murder of Ralph Pitsen, street name Piss. Known associates include these four men." Another slide. "One is currently serving time for armed robbery. These two"—he used a laser pointer—"are believed to be out-of-province. This man, Danny Dipietro, was spotted in Rivermede last week. His current whereabouts are unknown."

Rip moved to a slide of a house, a long and low dingy gray-brick building. "Current domicile. Two story, unattached, isolated, nearest neighbors are eighty meters west and one hundred meters east. Four entry points. Front door, solid with two glass panels on either side, no screen. At the back, sliding glass doors. One glass panel is boarded up. No bars on the remaining glass panel." He flashed slides of the exterior of the house. "Attached garage with an exit from the house to the garage, located here. Exit from the garage, likely a metal door, located here." He pointed to a door off the right side of the house. He changed slides. "Last entry is a single wooden door in the new addition on the first floor to the west." He looked at the men. "According to our intel, this is the room where all the deals go down. The informant wasn't sure if it's also used as his bedroom." He pointed to the windows with a laser pointer. "Windows—one bay window on the first floor and four on the second floor at the front. Three total at the back. Two on the garage wall, which are boarded up, and one on the west wall of the addition. We'll use that as an entry point." He changed slides again. "This is what we've got on the floor plan. Stairs to the right just inside the front door." Rip continued on with the details of the layout.

"The house has been under surveillance for the last twenty-four hours, and it appears Giuseppe is the only occupant. However, Dipietro may have entered the premises four days ago." Rip looked at the men.

"Sierra, you'll precede the stack and cover the north end and the sliding door entry. The shed located here will be your cover.

"We'll approach with two raid vans. Dub and Shirk will lead the stacks. Shirk will break and rake the orange alpha window and then post inside, followed by a full entry of the remainder of the team. Dub and his team will cover the front door. Ram the front door and enter, take the staircase right to the second floor. Shirk and his team will clear the first floor. The canine unit will be standing by in case the suspect flees or bolts out the garage door. That's the least likely scenario." Rip looked at the nodding heads. "Any questions?"

Rip glanced at his watch. "Okay, kit up and meet in the parking lot in thirty minutes."

The men filed out and Rip completed the paperwork. He contacted the detachment commander for the area to let him know what was going down and requested two uniforms to set up roadblocks. The incident commander was on his way in, the canine unit was standing by, and the tactical medical team with two paramedics was ready to go.

When the incident commander arrived, Rip briefed him and he approved and signed off on the plan.

Rip shrugged on a load-bearing vest over the body armor he wore and checked the contents. Radio, handcuffs, quick ties, gauze, extra magazine, Taser, pepper spray, flash bang, and hand gun. He slipped on the Eagle headset and tugged a boonie cap over top. He walked out to the parking lot with the commander, and they climbed into the Suburban. Rip set his balaclava and helmet along with a pair of night-vision goggles on the front seat beside him and made radio contact with the team in the raid vans.

At 3 a.m., in the pitch black of night, they pulled out of the parking lot. Rip and the incident commander led the way in the Suburban, two raid vans with the men and paramedics followed, the uniformed police officers were next, and the canine unit brought up the rear.

Rip pulled up to the periphery of the property and stopped. The raid vans pulled up behind him and when he received radio confirmation that the uniforms had the road blocked in either direction, he gave the signal for the vans to pull into the driveway.

"Sierras go," Rip said into his headset. Mac and the other Sierra Element member jumped out of the van with Shirk and his team close behind. They led the stack across the lawn toward the left corner of the house.

"Lights up," Rip said into the radio to the uniformed officers. Flashing red lights on the cruisers lit the street.

"Set." Rip heard from Mac, indicating they were in position.

"Dub go."

"Copy." Dub and his team jumped out of the van and in a controlled fast walk made their way to the front door.

"Shirk, snap and crackle," Rip said into the headset.

Rip heard the tap of his reply, followed quickly by the sound of glass shattering with the break and rake and the quiet thud when Shirk landed inside.

"Police. Put your hands in the air," Shirk shouted. The three team members with him would follow him through the window.

"Dub, pop." Rip gave the signal for the front door breach.

"Suspect secure," Shirk said into his headset.

"Alpha blue clear."

"Alpha green clear."

"In and up," Dub said.

Rip counted out the time to mount the stairs and listened as they made their way through the second floor and cleared each room.

"Beta clear."

"Accessing third entry." A pause. "The garage has been made into a living space. The door, alpha green is open."

As soon as Rip copied it through his headset, he heard footsteps running toward his vehicle.

"Canine unit, tic tac toe."

He flipped a switch on the dash and the front lawn flooded with a bright white light. A man bolted from the side of the driveway into the dense bush beside the house. Rip grabbed his goggles and spoke into his microphone. "Suspect spotted. Northeast quadrant heading east into the trees at the periphery of the property," he said as he left the vehicle and ran toward the trees. With the night vision goggles, he could see a flash of white as he followed.

"Suspect, male, five-eight, one hundred and fifty pounds. Wearing boxers. No visible weapon."

Rip could hear the canine unit getting closer as he ran through the bush and dodged the low branches. "Police! Stop!" he ordered.

The suspect jerked at the shout and looked over his shoulder and then turned back and ran smack into a tree. He bounced off and staggered.

Rip shook his head. "Idiot," he muttered under his breath. He aimed his weapon. "Get down on the ground. Hands on your head."

The dog and his handler ran up and stopped.

"I didn't do nothin'," the male suspect said.

The dog growled.

The male swore and raised his hands above his head. He fell to his knees and then went face down on the forest floor.

"Good choice." Rip holstered his weapon and pulled out restraints. "We have a problem with the company you keep." He cuffed his wrists and hauled him up. "Let's go." He started walking back and spoke into his headset. "Suspect secure."

"Premises secure, Ripper."

"Copy." He spoke into his radio. "Residence secure. Send in the investigators."

The drug unit detectives met Rip as he headed up the driveway.

"Mr. Danny Dipietro, we meet again," one of them said as Rip handed the suspect over.

"I didn't do nothin'."

The detective smirked at Rip and took Danny by the arm.

"I'll need those cuffs back," Rip called after him.

The detective waved and headed into the house.

Rip walked over and joined the rest of the team near the raid vans. "Good job, everyone. That was quick and painless. We can debrief at the station."

The team loaded into the vans, and Rip drove with the commander back to the office in his Suburban. After debriefing, he let the men go and sat down to write the report. As the sun came up and the office started to buzz with the day shift, Rip was ready to head home for some sleep. Another warrant was coming down the pipes, but it looked like it would be forty-eight hours before anything happened.

He smothered a yawn and thought about grabbing another coffee. But a few hours of sleep would probably do him good. It'd be even better if he could wake up to Chloe.

He picked up his phone to text her. *Hey, you free today?*

He was at his car when she replied. *Working 'til 4.*

He'd be sleeping alone, but . . . *Would you like to go out for dinner?*

*Love to.*

*I'll pick you up at 6.*

*Perfect. See you then.*

Home. Sleep. And sweet dreams.

# Chapter 21

At six o'clock, Chloe heard a knock at her door. She had been listening for her phone to ring so she could buzz Rip into the apartment building. She set down the curling iron and gave her newly styled curls a last fluff and then skipped out to the living room. The bright pink skirt she wore flounced around her thighs as she stopped and pulled open the door.

Her heart tattooed as she looked into Rip's smiling eyes.

He handed her a bouquet of purple forget-me-nots and leaned down to kiss her. Chloe caught the scent of fresh soap. Her eyes fluttered open as he pulled back. "Hi," she said softly.

"Hi. I slipped in the front door with the pizza delivery guy. Your building security needs a bit of work," he said. He brushed her curls. "You look beautiful. I love the curls."

Chloe's smile widened. "Thank you. Most men wouldn't have noticed."

"Well, I am a trained observer," he said with a grin.

Chloe laughed and sniffed the bouquet she held. "Thank you for the flowers. I'll just put them in water and grab my sweater."

"Bring a swimsuit, and we can go back to my place and use the hot tub later."

Chloe paused, looking over her shoulder at him. "Do I need a swimsuit?"

Rip's eyebrows went up, and his eyes flared with interest. "You know, I've always said we could save a lot of money if we didn't have to worry about clothes."

"It'd probably be better for the environment, too." Chloe grabbed her sweater and purse and moved toward the door.

"Absolutely. And think how much easier travel would be."

They stepped out into the hallway, and Chloe locked the door. "No need to fuss about the best swimsuit to fit your shape," she said as they walked toward the elevator.

"The time it would free up. No more busy shopping malls." He took Chloe's hand in his.

"Although, it might be awkward sitting with your buddies at the bar," Chloe pointed out.

Rip nodded. "True. There is that. And camouflage might be a problem."

"Hmmm. Paint spatters everywhere," Chloe said as the elevator doors opened. "I'm not the neatest painter."

Rip pulled her close as they stood at the back of the elevator. "I could help with the hard-to-reach spots," he whispered in her ear.

Chloe felt a flutter in her belly. "So many pros, so few cons. I think we're on to something."

Rip chuckled. "I've never looked more forward to the end of an evening," he said, looking into her eyes.

The elevator doors opened, and Rip guided her gently with a hand on the small of her back. A sweet swirl of emotion caught Chloe's breath at the warmth of his touch.

He opened the door to the building and motioned for her to go first. "The car's this way." He took her hand again and brushed his thumb across her palm.

Chloe spotted the Miata in the parking lot. "Oooh. The convertible." She looked up at him. "If there wasn't a promise of a hot tub waiting, I'd suggest we take the long route."

Rip brought her hand up for a quick kiss. "You know, I'm not even hungry."

She looked up at his eyes and then roamed down his body. The light blue T-shirt looked soft against the hard muscles of his shoulders and chest. Faded jeans hugged his hips and the bulge across the front was very appealing.

Chloe brushed against him. "Whoever invented takeout was a genius."

Rip bent to kiss her and then stopped. "If I start, I won't want to stop." He opened the car door, and Chloe hopped in. He came around and sat beside her.

"McDonald's would be the fastest," she said as she watched him.

"I was thinking delivery."

Chloe waved her hands. "Even better. I like a man with a plan." Plan. Plan. Oh, she groaned. She wasn't supposed to have sex. Shit. She wasn't thinking. Hormone heaven made her mind misty. "Ah, Rip. Wait. Wait. Ah, I forgot. I can't have sex right now. It's the wrong time of the month."

Rip's head whipped around and the car slowed. "What?"

"I'm sorry. Really sorry," she said, lifting her hands and lowering them to her lap. "Can I take a rain check for seven days from now?"

She watched as understanding flashed across his face. He leaned his head back briefly and glanced over at her. "Really?"

"Sorry. Yes. Really."

He sighed. "Of course. Seven days, eh? What's that? Thursday. First thing in the morning? Do you get a lunch break? Or should I pick you up from work?"

She smiled. "Sounds like a great way to start the day."

His shoulders relaxed and he nodded. "We have reservations at Harper's. We could still make it." He looked over at her with a question in his eyes.

She looked at him, loving him even more. "Sounds lovely. Not as good as plan A. But not a bad plan B. And maybe we could take the long route."

Chloe leaned back and wiped her napkin across her lips. "That was delicious." Her plate was clean and the wine glass nearly empty. The causal atmosphere of the family-owned restaurant belied the five-star meal.

Their table by the window overlooked the lake, and Chloe watched as a sailboat maneuvered into its slip at the nearby marina. "I wonder how hard it is to do that?"

Rip followed her gaze. "Pull a boat into a parking spot?"

"Yeah."

"It's probably like riding a bicycle. Except the bike is really long and the ground shifts underneath as you ride."

Chloe laughed. "They make it look easy. I love watching the water."

Rip nodded. "It's calm tonight. There's a path along the waterfront. Would you like to go for a walk? They rent rollerblades, too. We could go for a spin."

She sat up. "I'd love that."

Chloe finished her wine as Rip paid the bill. They walked outside, along the sidewalk around the restaurant, down to the marina. A small shop out front handled the rentals and an older gentleman, skin wrinkled and deeply tanned, watched them approach.

Rip turned to Chloe. "Have you rollerbladed before?"

"Not in a while. But the advantage of being the youngest of six is the hand-me-downs. We had every sport covered. I think it was Devon who begged for a pair of rollerblades one Christmas. By the time the snow melted, he'd already outgrown them, but they were a perfect fit for me. I wore them all summer. Even had visions of making it to the Olympics."

"Wow. Big dream."

"Yes, if it actually was an Olympic sport, I'd have done quite well."

They shared a laugh and exchanged their shoes for rollerblades and helmets.

"We close at nine so you have an hour," the older gentleman said as he set their shoes in a bin and handed them a ticket. "If you head out that way," he said, pointing away from the restaurant, "you'll have the best view of the sunset. I think we're in for a show tonight."

Chloe and Rip headed out in the direction he suggested. They held hands and synchronized the rhythm of their skating, at a leisurely pace.

Chloe looked over at Rip and watched him move. "You look like you've done this before, too."

He shrugged. "I've played a lot of hockey and this is pretty close. Luckily, it's flat because I'm not sure a hockey stop would work."

The boardwalk was quiet except for an occasional jogger. Chloe smiled at a young couple pushing a stroller. "I'm going to do that," she said to Rip as they passed.

Rip looked around. "Do what?"

"Take my baby for a walk every evening. I've heard it's very healthy to expose the baby to pollutants so they don't develop allergies. Dust, lake air, there's probably a bit of bird dander here, too, eh?"

Rip looked at her with raised eyebrows.

"You know, like sea gulls . . ."

"Are you pregnant?"

"No, not yet. But I like to have everything perfectly planned. So when I do get pregnant and have a little bambino, I've got all my ducks in a row."

They skated a bit farther in silence.

"So having a baby is important to you?" Rip asked.

"Yes," she said with a brisk nod. "Maybe I should visit pets when I'm pregnant, too. Eat peanut butter. I should make a list."

"Walk on the wild side."

"Nothing risky. But if you want to give your baby a head start, you have to begin early."

"Isn't that a long way off? I mean, what if you don't have kids? What if you change your mind or realize, you know, you can't have them?"

"I don't think that's going to be an issue. I've given it a lot of thought. I can't see changing my mind now." She squeezed Rip's hand. "Hey, don't look so sad. Really, it's a good plan."

Rip gave a small smile. "I think you'll make a wonderful mom."

Chloe beamed at him. "Thank you."

Rip nodded and glanced at the sky. "We should turn back. The sun is getting low. He's right—it's quite the show."

The sun blazed at the edge of the horizon and pink, yellow, and a luminous orange streaked across the sky. A massive weeping willow at the edge of the lake looked black in the low light and contrasted with the brilliant colors.

"What's that saying? 'Pink sky at night, sailor's fright. Pink sky at dawn, sailors be gone.'"

"Actually, I think it's the opposite. 'Red sky at night, sailor's delight. Red sky at morning, sailors take warning.'"

"Oh." Chloe laughed. "Good thing I'm not a sailor."

They made it back to the rental shop with five minutes to spare, as the sun dipped below the horizon.

"That was really fun," Chloe said, linking her arm in Rip's as they strolled back to the car. "You know what would be good right now?"

"Ice cream?"

"Yes, that would be good, but I was thinking of a soak in the hot tub." They reached the car.

Rip went to open her door, but turned to look at her. "Going in the hot tub's okay?"

"Yes. I can't do the big S, but I could do the little s."

"I have no idea what that is, but I'm game."

She laughed. "I think you're going to like it."

# Chapter 22

They made it in the door of Rip's house, and after one hot kiss, lifted their shirts over their heads. By the time they reached the bedroom, their clothes were shed and their hands busy. Sateen sheets and a light duvet felt cool against their naked skin.

Chloe explored every inch of Rip's body. Soft and smooth against the hard muscle. When he tried to change positions, she protested. "Uh, uh, uh. Me first," she whispered. She replaced her hands with her tongue and lips and explored. Sweet and musky, then salty and slick. She picked up the pace and strained against him when his hands roamed restlessly.

When he tensed and finally let go, she slid, brushing her breasts across his chest, and cuddled into his side. Rip held her tight, and she listened to his heartbeat slow. After a few minutes, he gently pushed her onto her back, kissed her lips and whispered, "My turn."

Chloe floated as Rip's fingers roamed. A light touch across her nipple, a line down her belly to the ticklish spot at her waist. Across the smooth skin of her hip, the sensitive area behind her knee, brushing her calves down to an erotic massage of her instep, and a leisurely trail back again. Sensation built from her head to her toes and when he closed his mouth around her breast, she strained to be closer.

She groaned as his tongue laved her skin and started the journey again, nipping and kissing. Chloe opened for him as his fingers danced lower, his mouth busy with her breast. The onslaught of sensation ripped through her, and Chloe clung to his shoulders and let the waves subside.

Rip kissed her and gathered her close. "I'm a huge fan of little s."

As her muscles relaxed, Chloe opened one eye and looked at Rip. "Can't imagine what big S is going to be like if that was little s."

Rip chuckled. "Thursday will be a good day." He kissed her. "Would you like to go in the hot tub now?"

"Love to. Not sure I can move yet, though."

"No problem." Rip stood and Chloe stared at his hot bod. Wowza. So many rippling muscles and an impressive sight below the waist.

Rip reached down and lifted Chloe into his arms. "You're as light as a feather."

Chloe's breath caught. "That will get you more little s." She kissed his neck. "You're built. And beautiful."

Rip smiled at her. "Right back 'atch ya." Rip set her down beside the hot tub and held her hand as she climbed in. "I'll grab a couple of towels."

Chloe slid into the water and leaned back against the side, relaxing. Rip returned and handed her a glass of wine. He had towels tucked under his arm and tossed them beside the hot tub before setting his own glass of wine down and climbing in. He brushed his lips against hers before he settled in the water.

Chloe sighed. "It's so quiet and peaceful back here. And look at all the stars."

Rip looked up at the sky and then over to her. "It's a perfect night."

They sipped their wine and relaxed, listening to the sounds of crickets chirping, and chatted about travel and places they wanted to visit.

Rip finished his wine and set his glass on the ledge. He turned to Chloe. "You are the most beautiful woman I've ever seen."

Chloe smiled. "And have you seen many?"

Before he could answer, his phone went off in the kitchen. He listened and then tensed. He took Chloe's glass and whispered in her ear. "We need to get out. That's the house alarm." He held Chloe's arm and guided her out of the tub. He handed her a towel as he moved her along into the house. "Head to the bedroom and lock yourself in the bathroom there. I'll check this out."

Chloe dashed off to the bedroom clutching a towel against her chest. Rip looked at his phone and saw that someone had been at the front door and had moved along the east side toward the fence. The gate had been shaken, which probably set off the alarm.

Rip set his phone down and went out the back door. He crouched beside the hot tub and listened. The night was quiet, but a rustling behind the fence had him tensing. He dashed to the gate and paused. As he opened it, the lock clicked. Running footsteps pounded the ground away from the fence toward the front of the house. Rip slipped through the gate and started chase.

"Stop! Police!" he shouted.

The suspect stopped abruptly and raised his hands in the air. "I come in peace," he blurted.

Rip slid to a stop. "Get down on the ground."

"Of course. Of course. Don't shoot. I didn't mean any harm." The intruder buckled, went down on his knees, and fell to the ground.

Rip approached him and pulled his arms behind his back.

The man grunted. "Please, I can explain. I think there's been a misunderstanding."

"Jared?" Chloe asked, her voice rising.

"Chloe?" Jared asked, perking up at the sound of Chloe's voice.

Rip put a knee against the man and held him still. Chloe appeared at the gate, dressed again.

"Stay there, Chloe," Rip instructed. "You know this guy?" he added, when she stopped.

"Yes." She put her hands on her hips. "Jared, what are you doing here?"

Jared struggled to get up. "I want my sperm back."

# Chapter 23

"What?" Rip asked.

Chloe looked at the two of them, staring back at her. Rip, naked and magnificent, looking calm and dangerous as he pinned Jared to the ground. He probably could use a pocket or two for handcuffs or a weapon, but man, she'd stop for that any day.

And Jared. She shook her head. Silly boy. All he had to do was ask for his sperm. She told him she'd give it back. What the heck was he doing?

Jared struggled. "I can explain."

"I know him, Rip. You can let him up. He's harmless."

"Hey," Jared protested.

Rip looked at him, but didn't move.

Jared sighed. "All right, I'm harmless," he agreed. "I'm a medical student, for Chrissake."

"It's true. He's a medical student," Chloe said.

"How'd you trace her here?"

"I got the address from her car registration. You know, the convertible. The top was down when it was parked at the sperm bank. I was worried I didn't have any contact information—"

"Is that true?" Rip asked Chloe.

"Probably. I drove the car to work and I might have left the top down in the parking lot. You should keep the glove compartment locked," she said to Rip.

Rip shook his head. "All right. I'll let go. You can sit up, but stay on the ground. Move slowly." Rip took a step to the side and then stood between Jared and Chloe.

Chloe walked closer and touched Rip's arm.

Jared rolled over and sat on the ground. He brushed hair out of his eyes and looked briefly at Rip before focusing on Chloe. "I'd like my sperm back."

Chloe's heart sank. "I told you I'd give it back. Why didn't you just drop by the sperm bank?"

"What?" Rip interjected.

"I did go there, but you weren't working and they couldn't find it. You haven't used it, have you?"

"No, it's scheduled for next Wednesday."

"What?" Rip turned and looked at her with his hands on his hips.

Jared started to scramble to his feet.

"On the ground, buddy," Rip growled.

Jared plopped back down. "You can't use it. Please, I need it back. I've changed my mind."

"Oh Jared." Chloe sighed. "Of course I'll give it back. Are you sure, though? I did a lot of research and you have the best sperm. I really think we'd make beautiful babies."

"What?" Rip asked again.

Chloe turned to look at Rip. He stared at her with a frown.

"Can I talk to Jared for a minute?" she asked. "Alone?"

Rip looked from Chloe to Jared and back. "I'll get dressed. Shout if you need me, Chloe." He glared at Jared. "We're not done." He strode through the gate into the backyard.

Jared stood up and stuffed his hands in his pockets. "Shit. He's a scary dude."

"You're the scary one. You come here like a crazy person shouting about your sperm. Jeez, Jared. What were you thinking?"

"I know. I know. But I couldn't get ahold of you. I regret this whole thing. I never should have donated in the first place."

Chloe sighed. "Maybe things have changed in your life, but you shouldn't regret it. A lot of couples wouldn't have families except for people like you. I know I'm disappointed I can't use your sperm."

He looked at her with sad eyes. "I'm sorry, Chloe. Very sorry. But I can't go through with it now that my dad is in the public eye. If anyone found out . . ."

"I know. I get it. But sneaking around at night trying to find me isn't exactly the way to stay under the radar."

Jared winced. "I was trying to keep it quiet. I wasn't sure how much your husband knew. I thought maybe I could talk to you quietly."

*Husband? That had a nice ring to it.* Chloe threw her hands in the air. "At night? In the dark?"

"Okay, okay." He stuffed his hands in his pockets. "Obviously, I didn't think it through. But I couldn't worry about it another night. It was already past the twenty-four hours you gave me." He took a breath. "I'm sorry." He glanced toward the house. "He seemed pretty upset. You didn't tell him?"

*No, you nincompoop.* But the last thing she wanted to do was discuss it with Jared. "I'll talk to Rip. You need to leave. Your sperm is packed in a container to keep it frozen, but I promise I won't use it. You can come to the sperm bank tomorrow and pick it up, or I can meet you somewhere."

"I could be at the sperm bank first thing tomorrow morning. 7 a.m.?"

"Fine. You're sure you won't change your mind?"

"Yes. I'm sure," he hollered.

"Hey," Rip said from behind them. He had changed into cargo pants and a T-shirt.

Jared started and held up his hands. "Sorry. Tomorrow morning at seven is fine." He looked at Rip. "Can I go now?"

"Chloe, any reason why I shouldn't book him and charge him with trespassing?"

Jared made a strangled sound.

Chloe stroked Rip's arm. "Truly, it was a misunderstanding."

"I don't want to see you around here ever again."

Jared nodded. "Absolutely. I have no interest whatsoever in being here."

Rip jerked his head in the direction of the road. "Fine. Go."

Jared turned and stumbled and then jogged toward the front of the house without a backward glance.

Rip turned to Chloe. "His sperm was the best you could find?"

# Chapter 24

Rip sat with his feet up on his coffee table and nursed a beer. Images flashed across his television screen. He should turn up the sound to listen, but he wasn't that interested.

So, Chloe wanted a baby and had insemination planned for next week.

After what's-his-face left, they had talked about it. She was after some sperm. To give her credit, she had looked horrified when he asked her if she would sleep with someone and lie about using birth control.

Apparently that was dishonest. And the lowest form of low. That was off the table.

He snorted. Going into private files at a sperm donor clinic was fine, though. She had protested about that and argued that she'd kept it confidential.

Shortly after that he'd called a cab for her. Said good-bye and shut the door.

He shook his head and took a sip of beer. Truth be told, it wasn't about her accessing his file. There were worse things. He really didn't care who knew.

No, it wasn't that.

He flicked through the channels restlessly.

Chloe wanted a baby. His mind circled round and round to that.

He always thought the big stumbling block hooking up with someone would be his job. Not everyone could handle the day in, day out stress of the TRU team. They kept the risks as low as they could, but realistically, the risk was never zero. That always worried him more than his ability to have kids.

He knew his fertility might be an issue. But at twenty-one and dealing with testicular cancer, he really didn't have much choice.

Whatever happened to love conquered all? He rested his head back against the sofa and tried to quell the queasiness in his gut.

Guess you had to let someone know you loved them first. He grimaced and took a swig of beer. He could handle snipers, raids, and hostage situations, but telling Chloe he loved her put the fear of God in him.

So what should come first? The 'I love you' or the 'I can't have kids because I'm sterile'?

He brushed a hand across his eyes. No getting around it. It's who he was. Take it or leave it.

He sighed. She might just leave it. That was the problem.

Between the surgery, radiation, and chemo, they couldn't guarantee he'd ever be able to have kids, so they suggested he set some sperm aside. Great advice, but the cost had been beyond what he could afford. He'd have been happy to stick them in his own freezer, but no, not allowed. Whatever. At that point, he'd been grateful to be alive.

In the end, a buddy had suggested using a sperm bank. Sperm storage for free. Seemed like a great idea. He found a clinic just outside of Rivermede that had been a little lax in their protocol, which totally worked in his favor. He figured it would be safe and sound. Surely, women seeking out donors would be more discerning than to use a hellhole of a sperm bank. Except he hadn't realized that they shipped all over the world. He'd been notified about a month ago that they were down to the last two of his samples and would he care to donate again?

He freaked, had the sperm shipped to Rivermede, and then paid to have it transferred to the hospital storage. So there were two vials of his sperm sitting in a deep freeze, but he had no idea whether they would actually do the trick. He sincerely doubted it.

And Chloe wanted a baby.

So it might be an issue.

He finished the beer and flicked off the television.

He should be content. He had his health. He was alive. He had a job he loved and buddies he worked with who would put their life on the line for him. The fact that he was shooting blanks should be the least of his problems. In fact, a time or two, it had come in handy.

If only he didn't get this ache in his heart when he thought of Chloe. Guess the first thing would be to talk to her. Maybe she'd be okay with a sperm donor. He rolled his eyes. Well, obviously she would. He'd have to get used to it. Or adoption. They could adopt.

He rubbed a hand over his face. Here he was plotting to make it work, making sure it was perfectly planned, and Chloe had no idea how he felt. Seemed a little ass backward. Then he thought of Chloe and smiled. She'd appreciate that.

# Chapter 25

Chloe pulled open the door of Mane Obsession and walked in. She stood for a moment and let the quiet chatter of two hairstylists at work and the hint of an orange blossom fragrance soothe her nerves.

She had met Jared at seven o'clock as planned and handed over his sperm. Reluctantly. Sadly. Her whole retirement plan out the window. Not to mention the cute little bambino that was never going to be. She sighed and then squared her shoulders. What was that saying? When a door slammed shut, it usually meant a window was open.

Hopefully not a basement window. And not at the top of a high-rise either, especially if she had to crawl through it.

She glanced at the woman behind the front desk and gave a little wave when she spotted Patriq walking toward her. It did her heart good when his face lit up, and he rushed over. How could you not feel sunny looking at the wide smile, the lime green T-shirt, and those bright orange pants?

He brushed jet-black hair from his eyes and reached out to hug her. "Chloe, my pet. Don't you look dazzling." He pulled back. "Wait." He stood straighter and squinted at her. "I see sad puppy eyes. Are those sad puppy eyes?"

Chloe gave a watery smile. "Maybe."

He took her hand and shook his head. "Well, let's see what we can do about that." He tilted his head at her. "Man-trouble?"

Chloe nodded.

Patriq tsked. "Don't you be getting wrinkles over a man. He ain't worth it." He led her to his salon chair in a quiet alcove at the back and gestured for her to sit down. He shook out a black cape and with a wide sweep, draped it over her shoulders and fastened it around her neck. "Sit back and relax. A little bit of pampering will do you good." He ran his fingers threw her hair. "This shade of Golden Retriever is perfect on you. Look what it does to your blue eyes. Are you loving it?" Without waiting for her to answer he continued, "If you're up for a change, we could go for an Irish Setter. Do you feel a little frisky?" He studied her in the mirror and tilted his head. "Maybe not. You had that recently, didn't you? What about a black Lab? With your pale skin, the black-Lab, Border-Collie look would be stunning. What do you think?"

Chloe looked at herself in the mirror. Was she up for a change? She hadn't tried black before. She looked at the dark circles under her eyes and frowned. Dark hair, black rings around her eyes. What if she ended up looking like a raccoon? "I'm not sure. The blond has been fun . . ."

Patriq nodded. "Don't go changing because of a man. We can perk this up, give you a nice shiny coat. You're perfect just the way you are." He gave a firm nod and stroked her head.

"Thank you Patriq. You're exactly what I needed today."

"Unconditional love—that's what it's all about it. I'm going to mix up your color. It'll just take a moment and then you can tell me all about it. Would you like some water?"

Chloe shook her head. "I'm fine. Thanks, Patriq."

She picked up a magazine and flipped through it while she waited. Man, she thought, looking at a curly do, it looked just like a Poodle.

Patriq returned, pulled a tray over, and set the bowl with the mix on it. He moved the foils within reach and picked up a comb. As he parted her hair into sections, he looked at her. "Talk to me, girl. Tell me your troubles."

Chloe gave a crooked grin. "Tomorrow was supposed to be the big day—"

"I remember. You booked the appointment today so you'd look fab for the announcement photos."

"Yeah. Well, there's been a bit of a snag with the sperm."

"No."

"Yes. After a lot of research I found the perfect sperm, but the sperm donor changed his mind."

"What? Can they do that?"

"Yup." Chloe sighed. "And then the backup donor, who is really hot, was peeved because I looked up his name at the sperm bank."

Patriq stopped brushing the colorant on the foil and frowned. "How else would you get his name? He should be flattered."

"I know," she said with wide eyes. "That's what I thought, too. And he says he doesn't want kids."

"What? No puppies? Yours would be adorable. Playful. Loving. Gorgeous. How could he not want that?"

"I don't know."

"You know, they say that men mature later. Not me, of course. I'm wise beyond my years," he said, resting his hand on his chest briefly and fluttering his eyelashes at her. "Could it be you sprung it on him and maybe, given time, he'll wise up?"

Chloe considered. "Maybe. He didn't say much. And he did seem a bit sad talking about it."

"There you go." He folded the edges of the foil and flipped it out of the way. "Trust your instincts. Sit and listen, and keep digging until you get what you want."

"If he'll sit down with me."

He looked at her in the mirror. "Call him. Go for a walk. What have you got to lose?"

"True."

"He'll come to his senses when he realizes what he's missing with you. Don't you worry." He picked up the next foil.

"Do you really think so?"

"I do. And I'm rarely wrong."

Chloe smiled. "Thanks, Patriq."

"My pleasure." He clipped the foils away from her face.

"Patriq?"

He stopped. "Yes?"

"Have you ever considered donating sperm?"

# Chapter 26

Later that afternoon, Chloe pulled into the parking lot of the convenience store and shut off the engine. She made her way inside and waved at Bea.

"Cute do, Chloe," Bea said with a smile.

Chloe brushed a hand through her bangs. "Thanks, Bea. I had it done this morning at Mane Obsession."

"I like it. That color is sunny and bright. You don't look too happy, though. Why the furrowed brow?"

Chloe mustered a smile. "Sorry." She thought of the rough go Bea had been through and told herself to snap out of it. She could choose another sperm. She could find another boyfriend.

Her heart ached. She just didn't want to. "I'm sorting out my life. And wondering when I'm going to win the lottery."

"Now don't you fret. Life will unfold as it should." Bea handed her a lottery ticket. "It's all a bit of a gamble."

Chloe took the ticket and handed over the money. "Thanks, Bea. You are so right."

She waved good-bye and with a lighter step, walked back to her car. It was all a matter of perspective.

Chloe pulled up in front of the apartment building and smiled at Taryn who looked as if she'd be floating on air except that her grandmother had a firm hold on her hand.

Chloe jumped out and came around the front of the car to help Helen and Taryn inside. "Hi, I hope you haven't been waiting too long."

"All afternoon," Taryn said promptly.

Chloe laughed. "Well, wait no more. Your chariot has arrived. I borrowed April and Scott's car so we could all fit. And you"—she tapped Taryn on the nose—"can use Ava's car seat."

"Yeah. We made some cookies for Ava," Taryn said, pointing to a bag Helen carried.

"Oh, she'll love them."

Chloe held the back door open and after Taryn scooted into the car seat, fastened a seatbelt around her. She closed the back door and opened the front so Helen could sit down.

"It's a bit low. Watch your head."

Helen folded herself inside and leaned to the center so Chloe could shut the door.

Chloe walked around and settled behind the wheel.

"Thank you very much for taking us today," Helen said. "This is such a treat. Taryn has been looking forward to it all day. Me, too."

Chloe grinned. "My pleasure. I'm going to stop and pick up Mom and Dad and then we'll drive to April and Scott's."

"And Ava's," Taryn piped up from the back.

"And Ava's," she agreed, glancing in the rearview mirror. "Ava was pretty excited about your visit, too."

They pulled into the driveway of the retirement home and parked in front of the doors. Chloe ran in while Helen and Taryn waited in the car.

Joy's face lit up when she saw Helen in the front seat. "Helen, so good to see you."

Chloe's parents climbed in the back beside Taryn. Joy patted Taryn's hand and gave her a side hug. "Look at you. I think you've grown."

Taryn beamed. "I have. My pink boots are too tight for me now. Grandma says she's going to put a brick on my head, so I don't get taller than her," she said with a grin.

Joy laughed. "I tried that with my kids, and it didn't work." She brushed Taryn's hair. "I think it made them grow taller. But then I had someone to reach the top shelves for me."

Helen twisted around from the front seat. "I never thought of that."

"Oh yeah. Embrace the height. It's very handy," Joy said with a laugh. She reached forward and squeezed Helen's shoulder. "How are you doing, Helen?"

"We're doing fine." She patted Joy's hand on her shoulder.

The drive to April and Scott's house passed quickly. When Chloe parked the car, Taryn unsnapped her seatbelt and jumped down. "Can I go ring the doorbell?" she asked.

"Yes, honey. Take the cookies with you, " Helen said, handing her the bag.

Chloe helped Helen out of the car, and Helen linked her arm with Joy's and they followed Taryn to the front door. Chloe joined her dad.

"How's your car running?" Hank asked, nodding to her car sitting in the driveway.

"Never gives me any trouble," Chloe said. "Like Old Reliable."

Her dad looked at her sideways. "You mean, Old Faithful?"

"Probably," she said with a shrug and a grin.

At the front door, Ava and Taryn were shrieking and jumping in each other's arms. April hugged Helen and Joy, and Scott strode over to shake Hank's hand.

"Come in," Scott said. He closed the door behind them and gestured toward the back. "It's still warm enough to sit out on the patio. Come on back."

"I'm going to show Taryn my doll," Ava said as she grabbed Taryn's hand and led her upstairs.

"Dinner in half an hour, Ava," April called after her.

"Will they be okay up there on their own?" Chloe asked.

"Oh yeah. Ava plays in her room all the time."

"There's nothing they can get into? Harmful chemicals? Toxic make-up? I hear the bathroom can be a minefield of poisons for children."

April laughed. "Relax. They'll be fine. Scott's going to get Dad to look at the car, and I'm sure Mom and Helen will sit and chat outside, so come and keep me company while I finish dinner."

Chloe followed her into the kitchen.

"I made iced tea. Would you like some?" April asked.

"Sounds lovely," Chloe said.

April reached into a cupboard behind her, pulled out a glass, and handed it to Chloe.

Chloe took it and glanced out the window. Scott handed a beer to her dad and they wandered off together around the side of the house. Helen and her mom sat on deck chairs under the shade of an umbrella sipping iced tea and laughing together. "What can I do to help?" she asked.

April handed her a cheese grater and a block of cheese.

"This is a great house," Chloe said as she grated the cheese.

"It's perfect for us. Good-sized backyard and a fifteen-minute commute to work. It's pretty handy."

"How does Scott like staying home with Ava?"

"They're both thriving. Ava starts kindergarten in another week. It's a half-day every day so Scott will have some time to work on his jewelry design, and still be home for Ava in the afternoon. I can't tell you what a relief it is not to have to worry about childcare."

Chloe nodded. It had been one of the first things she'd sorted out. If she couldn't afford childcare, there wouldn't be a bun in the oven.

"I guess I don't have to tell you about that, though. How's all that going? Isn't the big day next week?" April asked as she peeled an apple.

Chloe grunted. "It was supposed to be Wednesday, but I've run into a hitch with the sperm."

"Oh. How big of a hitch?" April pulled out a cutting board and started chopping the apple.

"Major. As in I don't have any. My ovaries are bouncing with eggs and there's not a swimmer in sight for them." Chloe felt her eyes fill.

"Wow. You had everything in place. I'm sorry, Chloe. That's got to be disappointing."

"Thanks April," she said quietly. "I'm bummed."

"You're working at the sperm bank tomorrow, aren't you? Look for another one."

"I could, but it took a lot of research to pick the right donor."

"Don't give up hope. I think you'd make a great mom. You'll find someone."

Chloe sighed. That was part of the problem. She'd found someone, and now the bar was set pretty high for sperm comparison shopping.

April pulled grapes out of the refrigerator and rinsed them.

"Here, I can help with those," Chloe offered. "You want them cut in half for the salad?" At April's nod, she pulled the cutting board toward her and picked up the knife. "Have you heard how Pam's doing?"

April measured out the ingredients for the salad dressing. "I think she's feeling a bit better. The morning sickness is easing up."

"Rough go. What about her and Rod? I was a bit shocked to hear she's pregnant. I thought things were a bit rocky there."

"I know. I was surprised, too. I don't think it was exactly planned. Pamela told me they're going to counseling together, and it's helped."

"I think she really wants it to work out."

"Ironically, they were arguing about getting pregnant," April said with a grimace.

"Yikes."

"He wanted a baby and she didn't."

"Seriously?"

"I think she felt she wouldn't make a good mom."

"Well, she is a tad rigid."

April smiled and poured the salad dressing in the bowl. She fished tongs out of a drawer. "I know, but Rod balances that out, and he's a good influence. I think she's coming to realize that she doesn't have to do it all herself. That she can lean on him. I think the counseling's actually given her more confidence. Last time I talked to her, she was a lot more excited about it. Even discussed baby names."

Chloe raised her eyebrows. "Well, good for her," she said quietly, trying to dampen the wave of longing that swept through her. "I hope it works out."

April nodded. "Rod loves her. That's a great start." She set the salad bowl aside. "Do you want to go check on the girls? The salads are done and the salmon has another five minutes. I'm going to set the table."

"Sure." Chloe snagged a piece of apple and popped it in her mouth. She went upstairs and followed the sound of voices to Ava's room.

"I think she'll wear this silver dress and those shoes to go visit her daddy," Taryn said.

"Where's her daddy?"

"At the halfway house."

"What's that?"

"Where he is when he's not home."

"Oh. Mommy must be at a halfway house when me and Daddy are home."

"So you can dress the mommy up."

"Okay."

Chloe poked her head in the room. Taryn and Ava were sitting on the floor in front of a dollhouse, each with a doll in their hands, sorting through clothing and tiny accessories.

"Wow. Beautiful playhouse, Ava," she said as she walked in. Both girls turned to look at her.

"Daddy built it."

"Nice. It's time to get washed up for dinner. Do you need to put this away before you come down?"

"No. We're still playing."

"You'll probably have a bit of time after dinner, so leave it for now. But Taryn, you'll have to help before we go."

"Okay."

Both girls jumped up and raced to the bathroom. Chloe watched Taryn mimic Ava as she washed and dried her hands. "All set?"

The girls nodded happily and skipped downstairs to the kitchen. April handed forks to Ava and napkins to

Taryn and put them to work. Chloe carried the salad to the table.

"Ava, can you go tell Daddy that dinner's ready? He's in the garage."

Joy and Helen came inside and when the men joined them, they settled around the table. They passed the food around and filled their plates. Chloe sat beside Taryn, helped her serve, and kept an eye on her as she watched the dynamic of a big family with wide-eyed wonder.

"You'll have to come and visit us," Helen said to Ava. "Maybe one afternoon, you could come over." She raised her eyebrows to April and Scott.

"Sounds great," Scott said. "One day next week would work or after Ava gets the routine of school down pat."

Taryn beamed. "You could bring your dolls."

Ava nodded. "Can we go play now? I'm all done."

April looked at Ava's plate which was mostly empty and over to Taryn's hopeful eyes. "All right. If you've had enough."

Taryn and Ava looked at each other and hopped down from their chairs. They held hands as they raced out of the room.

"So much energy on so little food. That's how we all should stay trim," Joy said with a laugh.

The adults finished their meals and enjoyed dessert and coffee.

When the sun started setting, Helen yawned. "Oh, excuse me," she said with a laugh as she covered her mouth. "I've taken to going to bed at the same time as Taryn. She's up with the birds, and it was easier to switch my schedule than hers."

Chloe's mom put her napkin on the table and touched Helen's hand. "We're the same. I like the early morning. It's quiet and peaceful."

Helen laughed. "I'll look forward to that. Not much quiet once Taryn opens her eyes." She looked at April and Scott. "Thank you so much for the invitation to dinner. The meal was delicious."

They cleared the table, and Scott shouted a five-minute warning to the kids. A few minutes later, they were in the front hallway saying their good-byes.

"All tidy up there?" Chloe asked as Taryn came down the stairs.

"Clean as a whistle," Taryn said.

Chloe's lips twitched. "Perfect." She turned to April and Scott. "Thanks for having us over."

"Any time. Keep me posted about this week," April said quietly in her ear as they hugged.

"Will do. I'll come back after I drop everyone off and switch cars." She looked at the group. "Ready to go?"

They nodded and walked out to the car. Chloe buckled Taryn's seatbelt and shut the car doors after her parents and Helen settled inside. They waved good-bye, and Chloe honked the horn as they turned out of the driveway.

Chloe escorted her parents back to their suite and gave a tight hug to Taryn when she dropped her and Helen off at their townhouse. They both looked ready to fall into bed.

She, on the other hand, felt restless and a bit sad. Every time she had to drop Taryn off, her heart cracked a little. It was hard not to envy April and Scott, or Pamela and Rod. Even Dale and Natalie, and Devon and Adrian. Her siblings had it together. Why couldn't she make it work? She couldn't even make a sperm donor stick. Jeez.

After exchanging cars, she drove back to her apartment. She let herself in and tossed her keys on the side table at the door. Toeing off her shoes, she absently flipped through the pile of mail on the table. The headlines on a parenting magazine caught her eye.

'Get your child to eat vegetables.' 'Discipline as easy as 1-2-3.' 'Loving your child is not enough.'

Really? Seemed like it would be a good start.

She threw the magazine on the table. Her enthusiasm was bruised, and she couldn't muster up the interest to read it.

She wandered into the living room and debated turning on her computer. It was only nine o'clock.

What would Rip be doing right about now? Probably at the baseball diamond or out with his team. Fighting crime. Saving lives.

She sighed.

She really missed him. His laugh. His solidness. The yummy body, of course. The whole 'I've got a man pinned to the ground with my knee in his back even though I'm buck naked and not even noticing' thing. It was pretty sexy.

Could she call him? And say what?

She could try, "You know, there's no criminal code for finding out someone's shoe size." Hmmm. Maybe there was.

What about, "You should be flattered. Your sperm was in the top two"?

Probably too competitive to appreciate that.

She flopped down on the sofa and leaned her head back. Why did it have to be so complicated? Why couldn't she just say, "Hey buddy, you're the one who donated sperm. What's the big deal?"

She closed her eyes. It needed a bit of work.

Five days. Five days to come up with another sperm sample. It could be done if she put her mind to it. She had done less in more time. Wait. She had done more with less time. Yeah. After all, how badly did she want it? She thought of Rip's sperm. And Rip. And choosing someone else.

Her heart sank. Five days may not be enough.

# Chapter 27

The following afternoon, Chloe sat at the reception desk at the sperm bank. It had been a busy morning, but it was close to the end of the day and the waiting room was empty.

She clicked around on the files, wondering if there was a sperm out there with her name on it. But nothing really appealed. She rested her chin in her hand and flipped from one file to another.

The phone rang, and she straightened and answered it. "Rivermede Sperm Bank. Chloe speaking."

"Oh Chloe, I had to call and share the good news," the voice gushed.

Chloe recognized the voice. Darla Spence had come in for sperm a few months back.

"I'm so excited. The sperm worked. I'm pregnant!"

Chloe's chest tightened. She wanted to be able to say that, too. "Congratulations Darla. That's fantastic. I'm so happy for you."

"Thank you. Alex and I are over the moon. I can't tell you. It's been such a roller coaster ride. We were afraid to hope, but the doctors are pretty confident it's all a go. I'm past the three month mark, and everything is looking good."

"Wow. That's awesome." Darla didn't get Rip's sperm, did she? She could look that up. "I'm glad it all worked out."

"Yes. I wanted to call and share the news with you. You were so helpful."

"Well, thank you. I appreciate that. Send us a picture when the little bambino pops out, and we'll pin it up on our honor roll wall."

Darla giggled. "I will. I so will. You have a great weekend."

"Thanks Darla. You, too." Chloe put the phone down, took a deep breath, and tried to brush the longing aside. She was going to have to do better. She couldn't work at a sperm bank and go through this every time she heard about a successful pregnancy.

She leaned back. What did she really want? She clicked on a few more files, but her heart wasn't in it. Why did it seem to take forever to get to the appointment date when she had sperm picked out and now, when she needed more time, it was approaching faster than a speeding train.

She sighed. Enough ruminating. It was almost three o'clock and time to tidy up and close. She was straightening the magazines in the waiting room, when her cell phone rang.

"Chloe? I'm so glad I got ahold of you."

"Helen, is everything okay? You sound upset."

"I'm at the hospital."

"What? Why?"

"It's the stupidest thing. I was cleaning out the kitchen cupboards this morning, and the little step stool I was on wobbled and toppled over, and I went down with it."

"Oh, no."

"Darn fool thing. Poor Taryn was home, and I couldn't get up. We called 911, and the ambulance came and brought me here. They're not sure if my hip is broken."

"Helen, I'm so sorry. That's terrible."

"They might have to operate."

Yikes. "Oh."

"If it's broken."

Chloe sat down. "When will you find out?"

"I don't know. They did an x-ray, but I'm waiting to hear what it showed. I can't walk on it, Chloe. Can't even stand on it. That can't be good. Even if it's not broken, they're talking about keeping me in."

"To make sure you're okay. What about Taryn? Is she with you?"

"I left her with the neighbor."

Poor thing. The sight of Grandma being carted off in an ambulance would've been scary. No Dad. No Grandma. She's probably frantic, too. "I can go and check on her. If she wants to come to my place, she can. Or I can move into your place until you're up and about again."

"Really?" Helen asked softly. Chloe could hear the tears.

"Of course, Helen. Don't worry. I'll look after her. And what about you? Do you need anything from home?"

"Yes, bless your heart." She rattled off a list of items.

"I'll go get that now. I'm just finishing at work. I wonder if Taryn could come and see you? It might help to reassure her. We could pick up the stuff you need from home and drop by for a brief visit. And by then, maybe you'll have heard."

"I would love that. You could ask her and see what she thinks. Oh Chloe, it's so disappointing. She was finally settling, the night terrors were gone, and now this."

"Can't be helped. And don't you worry about it. Focus on getting better. We'll keep our fingers crossed that the hip's just bruised and not broken."

"I hope so. I really hope so." She sighed.

"What's the code word this week?"

"Pink teddy, but she won't ask for it with you. You have the spare key?"

"Yes, I've got it. I'll go see Taryn, and either way I'll swing by the hospital and drop off what you need. Sounds like you've earned a two-night stay with them."

"Thank you, Chloe. I really appreciate it."

"You know it's no trouble. I'll see you shortly."

Chloe closed down the office and locked the door behind her. As she drove over, she thought about family. It was really hard when you didn't have any. What did you do? She had five siblings and her parents to rely on. And Rip. Even if he was a teensy bit angry with her, he would be a rock of support. But Helen had no one. Well, she had her. She was glad Helen had called.

# Chapter 28

When Chloe reached down and whispered the code word in Taryn's ear, Taryn threw her arms around Chloe's neck and burst into tears.

Chloe gathered her close and rubbed her back. "It's okay, Taryn. Grandma is going to be fine."

"They took her away in an ambulance," she said with a hiccup.

"I know, sweetie. You were a big help with that. You did exactly the right thing. Grandma's hip is sore, and she can't walk on it right now. But they're going to fix her up and make her better. Would you like to go see her?"

Taryn nodded.

"She asked if we could bring her a few things, so we'll gather them up from home and take them to her, okay?" Chloe pulled back and brushed the tears from Taryn's cheeks. "You could draw a picture for her while I get the stuff together. She'd like that."

Chloe thanked the neighbor and taking Taryn's hand in hers, they walked next door and let themselves in. Taryn sat down in front of the coffee table in the living room with crayons and paper, and Chloe went into the kitchen. She picked up the stepping stool and quickly put things back to right. No need for Taryn to be reminded of the fall.

She gathered the items that Helen had requested and put them in a bag. When she finished, Taryn came over to show her the picture. She had drawn her grandmother standing in a row of flowers and a heart with 'love Taryn' printed inside.

Chloe blinked back tears and gave Taryn a hug. "Grandma's going to love that."

The trip to the hospital was quick. When they arrived in the Emergency Department, Taryn slipped her hand into Chloe's. Chloe looked down at her pale face and scooped her up. "It's okay, love."

Helen was in a cubicle separated by a curtain, and they were allowed to go and see her.

"Knock, knock," Chloe said, peeking around the curtain.

"Chloe," Helen said, her smile widening. "And Taryn."

Chloe set Taryn down, and Taryn raced over and gave her grandma a hug from the side of the bed. Helen kissed the top of her head.

"I brought you a picture," Taryn said, handing it to Helen.

"Thank you, sweetheart. That's beautiful." She stroked Taryn's hair.

"Here are the things you asked for," Chloe said, holding up the bag.

"Thank you." A look of relief flashed across Helen's face. "It's just bruised."

"Oh, thank goodness. What great news."

"I know. They still want to keep me overnight, but no surgery." Helen gave a relieved smile.

"Perfect. Well, don't rush it. I can stay with Taryn, or she can stay at my place. It's not a problem."

"Yeah, a sleepover at your house," Taryn said, giving a little skip.

Chloe smiled at her. "My apartment it is." She bent down and kissed Helen's forehead. "Don't worry about us. I put some magazines in there for you, too."

"Thank you. I think I'll have a little nap. Whatever they gave me for pain is working wonders, but good thing I'm not driving."

Chloe laughed. "Try to rest. If you need anything else, call me. I'll check in tomorrow to see how you're doing."

Helen's eye's filled. "Thank you, Chloe."

Chloe squeezed her hand. "Get better." She turned to Taryn. "Give Grandma a kiss goodbye, and we'll be off."

Taryn reached up, softly kissed Helen's cheek and then turned to Chloe. Chloe's heart melted at the adoring look in her eyes.

"Have fun," Helen said.

Chloe looked at her and grinned. "My middle name," she said as she took Taryn's hand.

# Chapter 29

"These don't taste the same as Grandma's," Taryn said as she looked at the pasta and frowned.

Probably not. A half a cup of mashed carrots stirred in probably changed the taste of Kraft Dinner. "But they're good, right?" Chloe asked.

Taryn took another bite and chewed. "Yeah," she said finally.

With additional vitamin A and carotene. That's what moms did. "Try the chicken."

"No, thank you."

Chloe almost laughed at the polite but firm refusal. Oh well, maybe Taryn could have eggs for breakfast to squeak the protein in. Chloe's mom always said that as long as the kids got the equivalent of Canada's Food Guide over the course of a week, it didn't have to happen in every meal.

Taryn ate her last noodle and put her fork down. "Done."

Chloe smiled. "That's one clean bowl. Would you like some more?"

"No, thank you."

"Any room for dessert?" They had stopped at the grocery store on the way home. Chloe had picked up apples, carrots, and chicken. Taryn had chosen Kraft Dinner, ice cream, and sugar cones.

"I can get it." Taryn jumped up, set her bowl on the counter, and went over to the freezer. She grasped the door with two hands to open it and pulled out the carton of strawberry ripple. "Oh, it's cold." She handed it to Chloe.

Chloe opened the package of sugar cones, piled on two generous scoops of ice cream, and handed it to Taryn.

Eyes sparkling, Taryn took it. "Thank you."

They sat down again at the table, and Taryn ate the ice cream cone. Mostly.

As Chloe washed pink off the table, floor, and Taryn's fingertips to elbows, she asked, "Would you like to go to the park? It's still early, and it's nice outside."

There wasn't any hesitation. Shoes were on, laces tied, and they were out the door. They walked hand in hand down the street and around the corner to the park, with a quick stop to buy a lottery ticket. The park was a fair-sized green space with a climber and swings for little ones and benches and a lawn bowling area for the older ones.

As soon as they got near enough, Taryn recognized a little girl she had played with in the past and raced off to join in a game on the climber. Chloe followed more sedately and sat on the bench to watch.

A group of gray-haired folk played on the lawn bowling pitch (competitiveness does not diminish with age), a teenager walked his dog (that fur color would be perfect with her eyes), a baby sat in the sandbox eating sand (parent texting) and a young couple looking very much in love pushed a stroller (with a pang, she looked away).

Taryn climbed, chased, and laughed for an hour until sunset. They walked home and after a snack of cookies and milk, Taryn brushed her teeth, washed her hands and face, and climbed into Chloe's bed.

Chloe wrapped her arm around Taryn's shoulders as they read a story together.

Taryn yawned when they read the last page. Perfect timing. Chloe closed the book and stood up. "Time to tuck you in." She set the book on the nightstand and pulled the covers up as Taryn snuggled lower. "I'll be in the next room, Taryn." She kissed her forehead and shut off the light.

Before she had a chance to sit down in the living room, Taryn called her. She walked back and opened the door. "Yes, sweetheart?"

"Can I have a glass of water?"

"Of course." Chloe brought it to her and tucked her in again. She closed the door softly and settled on the sofa to read.

In the middle of the night, Taryn called out. By the time Chloe went to check on her, she had fallen back asleep. After that it was quiet.

They were up by eight o'clock and debating whether to have eggs, pancakes, or sugary cereal for breakfast.

"Pancakes," Taryn declared. "With jam and butter."

"Jam? What, no maple syrup?"

"I've never had maple syrup."

Chloe feigned shock. "Ya gotta try maple syrup. You're what, four? Yeah, I think you're old enough now."

They mixed the ingredients together, and Taryn set the table while Chloe flipped the pancakes in a skillet. With a heaping pile, they sat down to eat.

"This is yummy." Taryn licked maple syrup off her fingers.

"I know. It's a classic."

Taryn grinned. "Grandma needs to get this."

Uh-oh. "We can ask her. But it might be better to save it as a treat for here."

Taryn nodded happily. "Okay." She took another bite. "Maybe I could come next Sunday."

Chloe laughed. "Deal."

They finished the pancakes and cleared the table. Chloe washed the dishes, and Taryn picked out the cutlery to dry.

"Looks like a rainy day out there today," Chloe said as she wiped the table. "After we get dressed and brush our teeth, maybe we should give your grandma a call and see how she's doing."

Helen had a good night. She was waiting to hear from the doctor, but she was hoping to be discharged from the hospital that afternoon.

Chloe and Taryn spent the morning playing cards and dolls. Taryn drew another picture while Chloe made lunch. After they ate, they packed up and Chloe dropped Taryn off at the neighbor's, so she could pick up Helen from the hospital.

Helen was glad to be going home. They brought her to the exit in a wheelchair, but she was able to hobble to the car and into her townhouse. Chloe stayed the afternoon and made dinner with Taryn's help, while Helen napped. After dinner, she popped home for an overnight bag and went back to stay with them.

The following morning, Helen felt stronger and insisted Chloe could head to work. "Taryn and I will be fine. She's content to play on her own, and she has a friend a couple of doors down who'll take her for a bit this afternoon. Don't you worry."

Chloe was reluctant to leave her alone. "I'm going to be painting over at the Bennett's new subdivision today. I'll have my cell phone with me. I made a salad for lunch with the leftover chicken. It's in the fridge for you and Taryn. If you need anything, call, and I can be here in ten minutes. Are you sure you don't want me to call my mom? She could come over and stay with you for the day."

"That's a lovely offer, but not necessary. We'll be fine, really."

"You'll call me if you need anything?"

"Yes, I promise. I'm not too proud to ask for help."

Chloe relaxed. "Okay. I can stay again tonight. I'll make dinner."

"Chloe, you're an angel."

Chloe grinned and pretended to polish a halo above her head. She called out to Taryn. "Taryn, I'm heading out to work."

Taryn came running into the room and skidded to hug Chloe's legs.

"I'll be back around dinnertime," Chloe said. "You'll be good and take care of Grandma?"

Taryn nodded.

Chloe looked back at Helen. "Call me."

"I will. I promise. We'll be fine."

# Chapter 30

By Tuesday, Helen was back on her feet and well enough that Chloe could return to her apartment. To sleep in a bed. Oh, it was nice to be able to stretch out and roll over. And on Wednesday morning, Chloe was up early and off to the clinic. Today was THE day.

"Chloe Keay?"

Chloe looked up from playing Save QB! on her phone.

A nurse came into the waiting room holding a file and indicated that Chloe should follow her. "Right this way."

They walked down the hallway and the nurse stopped at the second room on the right. "Just in here. You can have a seat. The doctor will be with you shortly." She set the chart on the desk and walked out, closing the door behind her.

Chloe glanced around at the posters on the wall. Eww. She pulled out her cell phone, but before she had a chance to start playing the app, the door opened.

"Chloe, how are you?"

Chloe looked up. "Mikaela. I didn't expect to see you here today."

Mikaela smiled and sat across from Chloe. "We rotate through the specialty clinics as part of the ob-gyn residency. I've been working with Dr. Todd for the past four weeks and have another month with him. But if you're uncomfortable with it, there's another resident who could see you instead."

"No, not at all. It's the opposite. I'd rather talk to someone I know."

Mikaela nodded. "Perfect." She flipped open the file and then turned to the computer. "Let me bring up your information. I talked to Margo last week," she said absently as she clicked at the keyboard. "She was saying how grateful she is that you've taken on more with the painting."

"Ah, that's sweet. Only two months in, already in the full swing of things with the residency, and she still keeps tabs on the biz."

"She'd have a hard time letting go. She's been doing it for so many years. How do you find running the whole show?"

"Love it. Margo still helps with the contracts. That Bennett connection has come in handy."

Mikaela laughed. "I was teasing her about a wedding date. She'd like to plan for the summer, but I think it depends on her schedule. They might have to wait until the following year."

"When she's finished."

"Yes, exactly. If she can wait that long." Mikaela studied the screen and clicked.

"I'm meeting Margo for lunch tomorrow," Chloe said. "Would you like to come? I'm sure Margo would love to see you."

Mikaela looked up and smiled. "I'd love that."

"We're meeting at Widget's, at one."

"Oh, right beside the hospital. I could get away for half an hour. Are you sure, though? I don't want to interrupt if you and Margo have things to discuss."

Chloe waved that away. "Not at all. We're just keeping in touch. Come. It'll be fun."

"Lovely. Thanks for asking me." She turned the computer screen toward Chloe so she could see it. "I see you're scheduled for insemination today."

Chloe nodded. "That was the plan, but I've had a bit of a setback with the sperm."

"The sample didn't arrive in time?"

"Kind of. I picked two samples, but one wasn't available by the time I made the decision, and the other one was pulled from the stock."

"Oh, that's unfortunate. Are you going to wait to see if you can get it again? Once the donor is screened and approved, the next round of donations is usually quicker."

"No, I don't think that'll be the case with this particular donor." Chloe frowned. "I was going to cancel the appointment, but I wondered if there are any other options."

"We could help you find another donor. We're connected to a pretty extensive sperm bank here."

Chloe raised her arms in frustration. "It's so tricky. They give you so little information."

Mikaela nodded sympathetically. "It's hard, I know. They cover the basics pretty well. Physical characteristics like height and skin color. And there's usually information about education and hobbies. And male pattern baldness. Surprisingly, that's given. But beyond that, it's not very informative."

"I know. What about the important stuff? Like how do they get along with their mom, nasally voice, skinny legs? I can think of a few more important traits I'd like to know."

Mikaela laughed. "There's a lot to consider."

Chloe sighed. "I think I'll have to do a bit more research. Unfortunately."

"You're wise to go slow. Make sure it's what you really want."

"Don't want to screw up two lives, eh?"

Mikaela shrugged and smiled. "Single parenting isn't for the faint of heart. I'll review this with Dr. Todd, but unless you have any specific questions for him, you probably don't need to wait around."

"No, I don't at the moment. I guess when I find sperm, I'd like to be able to come back."

"Certainly. We'll keep your file active. Give the office a call when you're ready. I'll make a note on the chart."

Chloe stood. "Thanks for your help, Mikaela. It's great to see you again. And tomorrow. Widget's. One o'clock. "

Mikaela smiled. "I'm looking forward to it. See you then. And good luck with all of this, too."

"Thanks."

# **Chapter 31**

Chloe returned home that night and flicked on lights as she let herself into her apartment. After her appointment, she had gone to work and stayed late. She had originally planned to take the day off, but changed her mind when she needed the distraction.

April and Scott had made arrangements to take Taryn to play with Ava for the afternoon and were going to feed her and bring back dinner for Helen. Chloe gave Helen a quick call. They hadn't returned yet, but Helen was content and enjoying the quiet.

Chloe wandered into the kitchen.

Buck up, she told herself. She could still do the whole sperm donor thing. At some point in time. She was healthy. Could afford it. Could afford time off. Had supportive family.

She pulled eggs from the fridge and cracked them into a bowl.

Yeah. Didn't matter. She was really bummed. She beat the eggs with a fork. It was time. She was so ready to be a mom. Confounded sperm.

She poured the eggs into a skillet and stirred them half-heartedly while they cooked.

It'd be easier if she was a plant. One that had both egg and sperm. She wouldn't need a donor. No insemination. No appointments. And her DNA twice over. How could you go wrong?

Maybe that'd be too much of a good thing.

She slid the eggs onto a plate and carried it to the table.

And then there was the retirement plan to think about. It was such a perfect plan. Foiled.

The eggs were bland. She picked at them and set her fork down.

The whole evening yawned in front of her.

The whole evening to ruminate. Yippee.

She could head out to O'Malley's or meet up with friends. But really, she just wanted to do nothing. And she'd rather do it with Rip.

That's what she craved. Just sitting around, passing the time together, doing nothing.

He'd get that, right? Maybe she could call him and ask him to be her nothing man. Would that be better than asking him to be her number two sperm donor?

The next day she walked into Widget's and spotted Margo and Mikaela at a table by the window. She had come directly from work and hoped there weren't too many paint specks in her hair.

When she walked over, Margo stood up to give her a hug. "Happy belated Birthday, Chloe."

"Thanks. Sorry I'm late," Chloe murmured as she greeted her.

"Not at all. I just got here and look who I ran into," Margo said.

"Long time, no see," Chloe said as Mikaela hugged her. "Mikaela was at the clinic yesterday," she said to Margo as they sat down.

Margo's eyebrows went up. "How'd it go?"

"It didn't." Chloe looked at her ruefully. "The sperm didn't work out."

Margo laid her hand on Chloe's. "Oh, Chloe, I'm sorry."

"Yeah, it stinks. But I haven't given up completely."

Margo squeezed her hand and nodded. "Good for you. I hope it works out."

"Thanks." Chloe opened the menu. "And how's it going with you? Busy back to medicine time?"

Margo gave a crooked smile. "It is. Two months done, twenty-two to go."

"The two months have gone by fast," Mikaela said.

"I know. I'm enjoying it, but the more I do, the more I'm hoping to balance it with painting."

"Miss me?" Chloe asked with a grin.

Margo laughed. "Absolutely. Medicine is rewarding and challenging, but I miss the creative side. If I haven't already told you, Chloe, I'm very grateful that you're keeping the business going. I couldn't do it without you."

"Just shower me with gold and riches, and we'll call it even," Chloe said with a grin.

"How 'bout I buy you lunch?"

"Deal," Chloe said, delighted.

The waiter came to take their orders. Chloe hadn't looked at the menu, but she ordered the soup and salad special with Mikaela and Margo.

"I've been busy, too," Chloe said as the waiter walked away. "Granted, most of the work is for Bennett homes."

Margo twisted the ring on her finger. "Handy, that."

"Any news about wedding plans?" Mikaela asked, raising her eyebrows.

"We've set a date for next summer," Margo said, looking at them with shining eyes.

"Woohoo!"

"Congratulations. That's so exciting."

Margo laughed. "Third Saturday in July. Trace finishes his exams in June, and I requested a week's holidays, and it was approved."

Mikaela leaned over and hugged her. "I'm so happy for you. I'll try to get it off."

Margo's eyes watered. "Thanks. You'd better because I'd like you to be my maid of honor." She turned to Chloe. "And you'll be a bridesmaid?"

"Oh, absolutely," said Chloe. "I'd love that."

"We're going to try to keep it small because I'll be planning it around school. But we didn't want to wait."

"I'm sure it will be perfectly planned," Chloe said with a smile.

"Let me know when you go dress shopping. I want to come," Mikaela said.

"You have wedding plans in your future?" Chloe teased.

"Well . . ."

"What? Tell," said Margo, leaning forward.

"I don't know. I met someone." She put her hand on her heart.

"Deets," Margo said, waving her hand.

"I met him at a party my parents hosted. Fancy place, fancy food, fancy dress. He introduced himself. He's kind of quiet, a bit mysterious, very sexy." She wiggled her eyebrows.

"What's his name?"

"Elliott. Elliott Thornhill."

"Sounds serious," said Margo.

Mikaela bit her lip. "I don't know. I guess I'll give it time and find out."

The waiter served their meals and refilled their water glasses.

"Can I ask you a question?" Chloe asked as she poked at her salad.

They both turned to look at her. "Sure. Go ahead."

"Do you guys want kids?"

Margo looked into the distance for a moment and then nodded. "I think so. Some day."

"Yeah, me too," Mikaela added. "Not right away but eventually. Why do you ask?" She picked up her spoon and tasted the soup.

Chloe sighed. "What would you do if your beau said he didn't want kids?"

"Ever?"

"Ever."

Margo shrugged. "Before I met Trace, I probably would've walked away. But now . . ." She paused. "I don't know. I love Trace, so somehow we'd have to make it work."

Mikaela nodded. "It definitely puts a strain on a relationship when one person wants a family and the other doesn't. It's slightly easier when one can't. At least then, they could look at other options."

Chloe grimaced. "I keep running into men who don't want babies. And I definitely do. So I wondered if it was just me." She stirred her soup slowly.

"I don't think so," Margo said. "That's what keeps the population going."

"But there are a lot of people out there who choose not to have kids for one reason or another, and they're perfectly happy with that choice," Mikaela said.

"Yeah. I'm not one of them," Chloe said ruefully.

They looked at her sympathetically, but Chloe changed the subject and asked Margo if she'd picked a venue and colors for her wedding. They had a lively discussion about what she wanted.

They finished eating and settled the bill.

"Thanks for treating, Margo," said Chloe.

"You're welcome. And Happy Birthday, too."

They hugged, and Mikaela and Margo hurried off toward the hospital. Chloe walked in the opposite direction toward her car.

As Chloe drove back to the Bennett subdivision, she thought about Rip.

She missed his smile, his easy company, that sexy bod.

Did she love him?

Her breath caught and an ache filled her chest. Looked like it.

More than the thought of having kids? She sighed. Looked like it.

Damn.

She was going to need a whole new retirement plan.

## Chapter 32

Two weeks later, on a Sunday afternoon, Chloe sat at her computer and wondered how she could bump into Rip.

Yesterday she had given notice at the sperm bank. She couldn't do it anymore. Her heart wasn't in the whole sperm donor plan. Whenever she tried to pick one, Rip's gorgeous eyes swam in front of her.

Kids or Rip? Rip or kids?

It was Rip every time.

She'd always have Taryn and all the nieces and nephews in her life, and she'd find ways to fill that nurturing instinct.

But life without Rip? She was pretty sure her heart was still beating, but it felt like there was a big empty hole in her chest. The longing to be with him hadn't diminished any since they'd last seen each other. She couldn't let it go, not yet.

So. New plan.

Run into Rip. Make him fall in love with her. Marry him. Live in a beautiful un-baby-proofed home and love every minute. Retire on lottery winnings.

It could work.

She needed something subtle. Where she could test the waters, sort out how he felt about her without the 'I really love you' pressure in his face. Kind of like, what did they call it? An intervention. Yeah, if their paths could 'intervene' that would be perfect.

She clicked around Rip's social media sites without much luck. It looked like the baseball season had ended, and he didn't have any big plans splashed over his page. Too bad.

Work? It's not like he was out patrolling for speeding tickets. Short of staging a hostage situation or getting caught in sniper crossfire, that was out.

Maybe she could give the police an updated statement about Giuseppe. He had been in the news, charged with drug trafficking and a bunch of other serious sounding offenses. Hope he looked good in an orange jumper. Merv and Millie were also mentioned—they were spared jail time, mainly because of the evidence they provided against Giuseppe. Sadly Presto was closed down, but the article hinted it might be temporary. She'd have to keep an eye out for the grand re-opening, hopefully with cheaper brownies.

She didn't exactly have anything new to add to the case, but she could float around and try to sweet-talk her way past the eight locked doors on the way to Rip's office. Hmmm. Probably not.

No friend of a friend, hanging out at the same gym, running into each other at the grocery store. She tsked. Trying to meet up with the man of your dreams wasn't as easy as it sounded.

Where would Rip hang out? She clicked a pensive beat with her mouse. She could stroll, ever so casually, past his house. In the hopes of . . . him gardening in his front lawn? Or maybe rattle his gate late at night. She could end up with him naked, pinning her to the ground. She grinned. That had potential.

What else did they do together? Rollerblading. Hot tubbing. O'Malley's. He did like the burger and fries at O'Malley's. And she was peckish. She checked her watch. It wasn't too late to head over and join in the Sunday night game of 'He said. She said.' Even if she didn't win over Rip, she had a pretty good chance of winning her dinner.

Rip slid down into the hot tub and sighed deeply. God it was good to be home. The last ten days had been grueling. He spent the first five out in the field with his team. Twice a year they went up north and practiced core skills they didn't use day-to-day but needed in their armamentaria. Rappelling, sharp shooting, search and rescue, hauling one-hundred-pound packs through the forest in the middle of the night—a TRU team iron man. The last five days he'd done it all again with potential new recruits. If you were going to be part of the elite of the elite, you had to prove you had what it took. He yawned. And that you could do it on very little sleep.

He sank deeper into the water and leaned his head against the headrest. Something about knowing you were in top physical shape was gratifying, but man it was good to be back. Sleeping in a cabin for ten nights was enough. He liked the comfort of his own bed.

He let his mind wander and his muscles relax.

He hadn't been in touch with Chloe for what, two weeks now? Three?

Whoever came up with 'out of sight, out of mind' didn't know what the hell they were talking about. It was a bunch of crock. She wasn't out of his mind at all.

If anything he'd have to go with 'absence makes the heart grow fonder.'

He sighed at the ache in his chest and shifted in the water. Hell.

He had to stop procrastinating and do something about it. Physical exertion over the past ten days eased the frustration, but he had to face it. Face her. Lay it on the table and see where it all landed.

It was Sunday. He needed to haul his ass over to O'Malley's and see if she was there playing 'He said. She said.' and winning pizza. If she wasn't, he'd have to come up with an alternate plan. But no more excuses, it was time to sort it out.

After another five minutes, he sighed and heaved himself out of the hot water.

Why did the past ten days seem like a piece of cake by comparison?

# Chapter 33

Rip walked into O'Malley's and looked around. There was a pretty good crowd for a Sunday night. A group of guys sat at the bar watching football on the big screen. More than half the tables were full and country music honky-tonked in the background.

He weaved around the tables and wandered toward the back. The scent of a bacon cheeseburger wafted up and his stomach grumbled.

And then he spotted her. Her back was toward him, but he recognized the blond hair, the shape of her neck, her laugh.

She sat at a table with another couple eating pizza. Rip recognized the male as Cam, the lucky one who enjoyed the weekend at the Bennett hotel.

As Rip approached the table, Chloe looked over her shoulder.

Surprise, then a guarded expression, reached her eyes as she stood up. "Rip, hi." She leaned over and wrapped her arms around his shoulders in a quick hug. Enough for him to take in her citrus scent and want more.

"Hi, Chloe. I hope I'm not interrupting." Lie.

"Of course not." She touched his arm and turned. "Do you remember Cam? And this is Genie."

Rip held out his hand to shake. "I do. Hi, Cam. Genie, pleased to meet you."

"It's a pleasure meeting you, too," Genie said with a sideways glance at Chloe. "Actually, Cam and I were just leaving—"

"No, we weren't," Cam protested. "I was going to have another slice of pizza."

Genie rolled her eyes and pulled Cam's arm. "You don't want to eat too late at night. Acid reflux and all that." She gave him a look.

Cam wiped his mouth with a napkin and stood up with a sigh. "Right. We'll settle our bill at the bar, Chloe. Thanks for sharing your pizza."

"No problem."

He turned to Rip. "Nice to see you again." He squeezed Chloe's shoulder. "We can stay if you want."

"Thanks Cam, but I'll be fine," she said.

Cam nodded and with his arm around Genie, walked to the bar.

"Care to join me?" Chloe asked with a slight smile, as she sat down.

"Love to." Rip pulled out a chair and sat beside her.

The waitress came over and started to clear away the empty dishes. She looked at Chloe and Rip. "Can I get you anything else?"

"A beer—whatever's on tap, a bacon cheeseburger, and sweet potato fries, please."

"Coming right up." She finished wiping the table and left them alone.

"So, fancy meeting you here," Chloe said with a question in her eyes.

"Thought I'd come and see if I could win a free pizza."

"You're a little late. I won it about thirty minutes ago."

Rip tilted his head. "Congrats."

"Thank you. Would you like a piece of the winnings?"

Rip laughed. "Thanks, but I'll wait for the burger."

Chloe nodded and took a sip of her beer.

Rip took a deep breath and leaned toward her. "I hoped you'd be here tonight."

Chloe stared at him.

"I wanted to see you." Rip cleared his throat. Where was that beer? "Sorry I haven't called in the last couple of weeks. I was out in the field."

"Doing brave and dangerous stuff?"

"Sort of," he said with a crooked grin. "A mix of field training and screening potential new recruits. I just got back."

The waitress set a beer and his meal in front of him. "Anything else I can get you?"

"Chloe? Another beer?" Rip asked.

"No." She picked it up to show him. "I've still got half of this one. Thanks."

The waitress nodded. "Holler if you need anything."

Rip picked up his beer and took a drink. "How was your week?" He took a bite of the burger to settle the worst of his hunger.

"Good. Busy. I'm still painting Bennett homes over in the new subdivision. I was looking after Taryn for a bit, too. You remember her? I take her to visit her dad."

"Yes, I remember."

She took one of his fries. "Her grandmother, Helen, fell and injured her hip."

"Is she okay?" He took a sip of beer.

"Yes. Luckily it was bruised and not broken, and she's back on her feet now."

"Good for her. A broken hip would keep her down and out for a while."

Chloe nodded. "She's amazing. I hope I have that spunk when I'm in my seventies."

Rip smiled. "I can't imagine you without spunk."

Chloe fluttered her lashes. "Thank you. I'll take that as a compliment."

"As it was meant to be." He finished off his burger.

Chloe looked at him with a hint of sadness in her eyes. "I'm glad you came tonight." She shifted her empty beer glass. "I've missed you."

Rip felt the pressure ease in his chest. "I missed you, too." He looked around at the crowd in the bar and wished for quiet. "Would you like to go for a walk?"

She nodded.

He paid the bill, and Chloe pulled a jacket on over her T-shirt.

The downtown core was quiet. They walked toward the waterfront. The air was cool, and already dark at nine o'clock, but the soft glow from a row of nautical lanterns lit the way. They strolled along the boardwalk.

"So, did you, you know, pick a sperm, and all that?" Rip asked.

Chloe tensed. "No." She let out a breath. "I didn't do it."

Rip looked at her. "You were so gung ho. What happened?"

Chloe shrugged. "I had second thoughts."

Rip's heart skipped a beat. "You changed your mind about wanting kids?"

"I think I'll always want them," she said slowly. "But I realized there were a lot of important things to consider."

Rip reached for her hand. "Like . . .?"

"Like whether you love someone," Chloe said softly.

Rip felt a surge of emotion that caught his breath. "Chloe?" He stopped and turned her to face him. "When you told me you were looking for a sperm donor, I was upset."

"I know, Rip. I really didn't mean any harm looking at your file."

"It wasn't that." He shoved his hands in his pockets. "When I was twenty-one, I was diagnosed with testicular cancer." He paused briefly at her indrawn breath, but then continued. "I had surgery, chemo, radiation."

"Oh my God, Rip." She stepped closer and hugged him tight.

"I'm fine, now." He held her for a moment and then pulled back. "Hey." He brushed the tears from her cheeks. "It's okay. I'm okay."

She looked at him with watery eyes, and he gathered her close again and rubbed her back. "The doctors gave me a clean bill of health. I should live 'til I'm old and gray."

She took a deep breath and let it out shakily. "Thank God."

He smiled against her hair and inhaled her sweet scent. "Let's walk, Chloe." He wrapped his arm around her shoulders and guided her along the path.

After a moment, Chloe spoke. "Is that why you had sperm at the sperm bank?"

He nodded. "Yeah. They weren't sure if I'd need it, but they advised me to freeze some. Unfortunately, it was expensive. So instead of leaving it at the hospital, I donated at an out-of-the-way, hole-in-the-wall sperm bank just outside of Rivermede. I had trouble finding it, so I figured it wouldn't get much traffic."

"Sounds like the place in Carlson. We've ordered sperm from them."

"That's what happened. Turns out they don't need to be visible because they ship their samples out. A few weeks ago, I was notified that my vials were running low. I had them shipped to the sperm bank here in Rivermede and then transferred them to the hospital."

"So you have sperm?"

"I do, Chloe. But they can't guarantee it'll work." He looked her in the eye. "I love you Chloe, but I may not be able to have kids. That's why I was upset."

Chloe looked at him with wide eyes. "You love me?"

"I do, and I want to spend the rest of my life with you."

She grinned from ear to ear. "And you'd want kids?"

He nodded. "We could try. I'm all into trying."

Chloe laughed and threw herself at him in a hug. "Me, too. I love you, Rip."

A wave of emotion gripped him. He closed his eyes and held her tight.

She rested her head against his shoulder. "I hope your sperm work out, Rip. But if it doesn't, we'll figure it out together. I've come up with some really good screening questions for sperm donors."

Rip laughed. "I love you, Chloe."

# Epilogue

Chloe sat beside Rip in the waiting room. "Did I tell you I got a post card from Bea?" she asked.

"No. Where did she decide to go in the end?"

"She couldn't decide, so she's island hopping for a month."

"Good for her. She was pretty excited when you won."

"We all were." She grinned up at him. "Even the store was excited. They couldn't believe the ticket you bought actually won the big bucks. Best birthday ever for me. Those last set of wishes are coming true."

"And what's your wish?" Rip asked.

"It's already come true." She squeezed his hand and the ring on her finger flashed in the light. "You. The wonderful memory of our wedding. All perfectly planned, if I do say so myself. And this." She rubbed her belly. "I knew your sperm would be hardy."

Rip laughed. "Glad to be of service."

A young woman in a white lab coat stepped into the room. "Mr. and Mrs. Logan? Hi, I'm Shelley. I'll be doing the ultrasound today if you'd like to come with me."

Chloe and Rip followed her into the examining room.

"Chloe, you can hop up on the table and lie down," Shelley said, pulling the ultrasound machine closer. "Is it okay if I lift up your shirt?" She adjusted a drape across Chloe's belly, squirted warm gel on one side, and moved the probe around. The screen was a blur of gray and black. "I'm not sure I'll be able to tell, but did you want to learn the gender of the babies?"

Chloe and Rip looked at her. "Babies?" they asked in unison.

Shelley looked flustered and checked the screen. "Ah, yes. No one's mentioned there are three?"

Rip's eyes went wide and Chloe laughed. "Three?"

"Three active heartbeats. You're having triplets."

Chloe looked at Rip with a huge grin. "It's a triple play."

Rip leaned over and kissed Chloe. "Three times the fun. I love you, Chloe."

"I love you, too."

# About the Author

Linda O'Connor started writing a few years ago when she needed a creative outlet other than subtly rearranging the displays at HomeSense. It turns out she loves writing romantic comedies and has a few more stories to tell. When not writing, she's a physician at an Urgent Care Clinic (well, even when she is writing she's a physician, and it shows up in her stories :D). She hangs out at www.lindaoconnor.net.

Laugh every day. Love every minute.